MYSTERY ON MAGNOLIA CIRCLE

KATE KLISE

Illustrations by Celia Krampien

SQUARE
FISH

FEIWEL AND FRIENDS
NEW YORK

SQUARE
FISH

An imprint of Macmillan Publishing Group, LLC
120 Broadway, New York, NY 10271 • mackids.com

Our books may be purchased in bulk for promotional, educational, or
business use. Please contact your local bookseller or the Macmillan
Corporate and Premium Sales Department at (800) 221-7945 ext. 5442
or by email at MacmillanSpecialMarkets@macmillan.com.

Library of Congress Cataloging-in-Publication Data is available.

Originally published in the United States by Feiwel and Friends
First Square Fish edition, 2022
Book designed by Mallory Grigg
Square Fish logo designed by Filomena Tuosto
Printed in the United States of America by Lakeside Book Company,
Harrisonburg, Virginia

ISBN 978-1-250-83305-1 (paperback)
10 9 8 7 6 5 4 3 2

AR: 4.1 / LEXILE: 620L

For Roger Kaza,

who helped me turn it around

◇◇◇

ONE

◇◇◇

I Hate Stairs

On the last day of school, I fell down the front steps of my house and broke my leg. After the surgery, my doctor said I'd have to wear a cast on my leg for most of the summer.

"You might think your world will get smaller," Dr. Ames said. "But depending on how you spend this time, your world could actually get bigger."

I rolled my eyes, but stopped when I heard Mom fake-clearing her throat.

"We appreciate your good care," Mom said to Dr. Ames. "Don't we, Ivy?"

We certainly did not. *We* did not appreciate anything or anyone because *we* knew what this meant. Spending the summer with my leg in a cast meant no bike riding around Forest Park. No swimming. No watersliding. No scootering. No practicing gymnastics in my backyard.

And I was expected to feel *appreciative*? *No, thank you.*

"I'm sending you home in a wheelchair," Dr. Ames said. "But I'd like you to start using crutches as soon as possible."

"Where do we get the crutches?" Mom asked.

"Third floor," Dr. Ames said. "Physical therapy. They'll fit Ivy for crutches and teach her how to use them."

He paused to make a sad-clown face. Then he pointed at my cast. It covered my entire left leg, from my foot to my upper thigh.

"I'm sure this isn't what you had in mind for summer, Ivy. But I know you'll make the most of it."

"Of course she will," said Mom.

"If I were you," Dr. Ames continued, "I'd spend this time learning something new. Not just how to walk with crutches, but something fun. A new skill, a language, coding. I hear coding's a terrific thing for kids to learn. You could take an online masterclass."

I started to roll my eyes again, but Mom gave me her aggressively fake smile.

"Now *there's* an idea," she said in a singsongy voice. "What do you think about taking an online masterclass, Ivy?"

What did I think? It was summer. *That's* what I thought.

I'd worked hard all year. I'd won the fourth-grade spelling bee *and* the fourth-grade multiplication bowl. I'd earned a perfect score on my Trojan War project, which was pretty impressive considering it was supposed to be a group project and my so-called partner, Melvin Moss, disappeared the day after we got the assignment.

More to the point: I didn't *want* to take an online masterclass. I'd spent most of third grade online. Besides, I already knew how to code.

"Whatever you do," Dr. Ames said, "think of this experience as an adventure. You're probably the only ten-year-old girl in your zip code with a minimally displaced fracture of the tibia and fibula just above the ankle. Write down what you learn on this journey. Capture the wisdom

with paper and pen. I think you'll find it a valuable exercise."

Mom was now looking at me with bugged-
out eyes as if to say, *Please, Ivy. Just be polite.
We'll stop for ice cream on the way home.*

So I said the only thing I could think of that
wouldn't be rude to the doctor but would also
convey how miserable I was and would be all
summer long.

"What I have learned so far on this journey,"
I said slowly, with bitter tears burning in my
eyes, "is that I *hate* stairs."

My street is shaped like a lollipop. Most of
Magnolia Circle is straight, but there's a loop
at the end where cars can turn around. Some
people call my street a cul-de-sac, which Dad

told me is French for "bottom (*cul*) of (*de*) a sack (*sac*)." It's a fancy way of saying *dead end*.

My family—it's just Mom, Dad, and me—uses the term *cul-de-sac* to mean any situation that leads nowhere.

The idea of spending the summer with a cast on my leg seemed like a cul-de-sac if ever there was one. My best friend agreed. Teddy Samuelson lives across the street in a four-story apartment building called Magnolia Manor.

The day after my surgery, Teddy came over with his dog, Lotty. It's short for Lottery. Teddy was so happy the day he got an Irish setter, he felt like he'd won the lottery. So he named the dog Lottery, which was quickly shortened to Lotty.

Lotty is best friends with my dog, Winthrop. He's a rescue sheepdog who looks like a distinguished professor in serious need of a haircut.

"Should I sign it?" Teddy asked, gesturing with his head at my bright green fiberglass cast.

I was sitting in the wheelchair feeling sorry for myself. My bad leg was propped up with pillows on a chair.

"I don't care," I said.

"I could write my name on it," Teddy said. "And Lotty's name, too, if you want."

"I don't care," I repeated.

"Or I could draw something," Teddy offered. "You always say I'm the best artist in fourth grade."

"Going on fifth grade," I said.

"I could draw Lotty and Winthrop," Teddy said. "I'd need to practice first, but I bet I could do it."

"Whatever."

I don't know why I was acting so crabby

toward Teddy. He was only trying to be nice. It wasn't his fault I was stuck inside my house for the summer.

"It's terrible about your leg," Teddy said, "but I have even worse news."

"Nothing's worse than this," I mumbled, crossing my arms and staring out the window.

"Mm-hmm," Teddy replied. He suddenly sounded like he might cry. His voice dropped to a whisper. "Something's wrong with Lotty."

I turned to look at Teddy's dog. "What's wrong with her?"

"She won't eat. She won't play. All she wants to do is sleep."

"Did you take her to Dr. Juniper?" I asked.

I knew Lotty's doctor because my family and Teddy's family used the same veterinarian,

Dr. Juniper. She's the vet my mom took her pets to when she was a kid.

"We went yesterday," Teddy said. "Dr. Juniper said she doesn't know what's wrong with Lotty. We have to go back on Monday. She wants to do tests. She'll probably have to draw more blood."

"Maybe it's the flu," I said. "Do dogs get the flu?"

Tears welled in Teddy's eyes. "I don't know. I just want her to be back to normal."

I knew the feeling.

"She can't even walk around the park," Teddy said, sniffling.

"I can't, either," I reminded him.

A few moments of silence passed as Teddy stroked Lotty and I scratched Winthrop's ears.

"Want to play gin rummy?" I finally said.

"Sure. I know where the cards are. Kitchen junk drawer, right?"

I didn't have time to say *right*. Teddy was back, shuffling the cards in a matter of seconds.

◇◇◇

What I learned from that:

Best friends know exactly
where you keep your cards.

◇◇◇

TWO

◇◇◇

Dogs and Dead Ends

*O*ur neighborhood was never especially inter-
esting. I always thought it was because we
didn't have a lot of kids on our street. It's mostly
older people who liked the combination of big
trees, medium-size houses, and small, shady yards.

But news that we were getting a street sign
created instant drama. In early June, someone
at St. Louis City Hall decided we needed a sign
that said *dead end* at the entrance to Magnolia
Circle.

Teddy was my source of all news on the subject.

"So," he said, on day five of our gin-rummy battle, "everyone on Magnolia Circle received a notice in the mail that said a dead-end sign would be installed on September first, 'barring significant opposition to the plan.'"

I pushed my wheelchair back a few inches from the table so I could evaluate my cards. "Does that mean we're getting the sign?" I asked.

"I'm not sure," Teddy said, looking at his cards. "My mom says the older people on our street like the idea of a dead-end sign because they think it will cut down on 'turnarounders.'"

Turnarounders is what we called people who turned down Magnolia Circle by mistake. When they realized the street was a dead end, they'd speed up, zip around the circle, and zoom away, as if there were something contagious about our quiet tree-lined street.

"And, of course," said Teddy, "everyone who lives in my building likes the idea of the sign because they say it'll mean more street parking for us. Our doorman, Joel, really wants the sign because he's really tired of people asking him to save parking spaces for them."

"Makes sense," I said.

Joel was the maintenance man in Teddy's apartment building, but he preferred to be called a doorman. I always loved the idea of a doorman. I wished we had someone at our house who said hello and goodbye to everyone as they were coming and going.

I bet my parents would also like a dead-end sign. We had a driveway next to our house, but my mom didn't like when her already stressed-out patients couldn't find a parking place on the street.

My mom's a psychiatrist with a small office in the back of our house where she sees patients. My dad's a cardiologist at the local veterans' hospital. Mom and Dad met and fell in love in medical school. They were partners in a class where they learned how to give medicine intra-venously, or through a vein, more commonly known as IV therapy. That's why they named me, their only child, Ivy.

"So is anybody *against* a dead-end sign?" I asked.

"Oh yeah," said Teddy. "Some people are dead set against it. Mr. Hobart says it'll bring down property values."

"Why?"

"He thinks the words *dead end* are depressing. Nobody wants to buy a house on a dead end."

"It means the same exact thing as a cul-de-sac," I said. "Except more people might actually know what *dead end* means." I snapped down three jacks. "Gin."

"Jeez," Teddy groaned. "That's the fourth game in a row you've won."

"You're not paying attention," I said. "Didn't you see I was collecting jacks?"

"My mind is mush today."

"You're worried about Lotty."

"Yeah."

Dr. Juniper had insisted Lotty spend another night at her clinic. The poor dog had already endured two full days of tests.

"Still no word on what's wrong with her?" I asked.

"Dr. Juniper doesn't know what it is," Teddy said. "I just hope it's not . . ."

"What?" I said, shuffling the cards for another game of rummy.

"You know," Teddy said quietly. "A *dead end.*"

I put the cards down on the table and looked at Teddy. "Lotty is the luckiest dog alive. And she's only three years old. She's not going to *die.*"

"I know," Teddy said. "Because if Lotty died, I don't know what I would do."

As if that were his cue, my dog, Winthrop, woke up from a nap and sauntered over to Teddy's side.

"See?" I said. "Even Winthrop knows Lotty's going to be okay. That's what he's trying to tell you."

Teddy massaged Winthrop's neck. "Such a sweet, chubby dog."

"Winthrop's not chubby!" I said.

"He will be if we don't start walking him again," Teddy said.

He was right. We used to take Winthrop and Lotty for a long walk around Forest Park every day after school.

"How am I supposed to walk with this stupid cast on my leg?" I said.

Teddy pointed at the crutches leaning against the wall. "What do you think those are for?"

"It's not as easy as you think," I grumped. "They hurt my arms. I can't do it."

"Have you tried?"

"Of course I tried! I mean, I kinda tried. Once. With the physical therapist at the hospital."

Teddy was already across the room. He was using my crutches to hop around.

"This is hard? Really? *This?* This is too hard for Miss Straight-A's Ivy?"

"Try doing it with a hundred-pound cast on your leg," I said.

"Your cast doesn't weigh a hundred pounds," Teddy said.

Before I knew it, he was pulling me out of the wheelchair and wedging the crutches under my armpits. "Come on. You can do this."

An hour later, we were outside with Winthrop.

The hardest part was getting down the front steps of my house. I hopped down each step on my good leg, with one arm on the iron handrail and the other arm wrapped around Teddy's neck.

"Am I strangling you?" I asked.

"Yes. But what're friends for?"

He made me laugh.

"You have no idea how hard this is," I said, panting and laughing at the same time. We were almost to the bottom.

"Just remember," Teddy said, grimacing, "you're doing this for Winthrop. He needs a good walk."

"Right," I said. "We'll do anything for our dogs."

I thought about saying something nice to reassure Teddy about Lotty, but I decided against it.

◇◇◇

What I learned from that:

*Sometimes it's better **not** to talk*

about things with friends, especially

if you know you're both worrying

about the same thing.

◇◇◇

THREE

◇◇◇

The Worst Possible News

Teddy called the next morning. His voice was trembling. "We have a family meeting today at Dr. Juniper's office."

"What's going on?" I asked.

"Dr. Juniper wants to talk about Lotty. It can't be good."

In my mind, I agreed. It sounded like the worst possible news, but I couldn't say that to Teddy.

"Daphne says Lotty's days are numbered," Teddy said.

Daphne would say that. She was Teddy's eighteen-year-old sister and was spending the summer reading tragic novels about teenagers with deadly diseases.

"Try not to catastrophize," I said, borrowing a word I'd heard my mom use. "That means try not to assume the worst-case scenario."

But the worst case was correct.

The family meeting with Dr. Juniper was scheduled for ten thirty. Just before noon, Teddy called me. He could barely talk.

"I . . . can't . . . even . . ."

"Tell me everything," I said.

Now he was crying hard. "I ... I ..."

"Do you want to come over?"

"No," he said. "I wouldn't be ... very good company."

"You think I care?"

"I can't believe it," he said in a whisper. "Dr. Juniper did blood work. The test results came back positive." His voice dropped. "Leukemia."

"Dogs can get *leukemia*?"

"Yeah," Teddy replied. "Canine leukemia." He took a deep breath. "Dr. Juniper said Lotty's a strong dog, but the leukemia is stronger."

"Unbelievable," I said. "It's just unbelievable."

"I know," Teddy said. "She said there are treatments, but they're crazy expensive and they don't always work."

"We have to try," I said. "We can earn the money—you and me, this summer. We can walk dogs. Er, *you* can walk dogs. I'll tutor little kids. I can help them with reading or multiplication tables or . . ."

Teddy started to cry again. "The treatment costs, like, *ten thousand dollars*. Mom and Dad are already worried about how they're going to pay for Daphne's college. She starts in August."

"I know, but we can—"

"No, we *can't*," Teddy said. He paused to blow his nose. "Dad's been trying to pick up more shifts at the factory, but it's not happening. Mom says her salon has lost twenty percent of their clients to those new hair-coloring-at-home products because they advertise twenty-four seven on the most popular podcasts."

"We can help your mom launch a marketing campaign for the salon. We'll think up some fun and cheap ways to—"

"You're not hearing me, Ivy. It's too late!"

There was nothing more to say. We stayed on the phone for a full minute, maybe two minutes, without speaking. "I can't believe it," I finally whispered. "Lotty."

"Lotty," Teddy repeated.

"So what does this mean?" I asked softly. "What did you do?"

"We all took turns saying goodbye," Teddy said. "I held her paw and told her what a good dog she'd been and how she'd always be part of our family. And then we left her with Dr. Juniper. She said we didn't have to stay till the bitter end."

"I . . . I can't even wrap my head around this."

"Me, neither," said Teddy. "But I know one thing for sure."

"What?"

"From now on, I want you to call me Ted."

"*What?* Where is this coming from?"

"I don't know. I just don't feel like a Teddy anymore. I feel more grown-up, like a Ted. That's what death does to you."

"Okay," I said solemnly.

"If you forget and call me Teddy once in a while, it's all right," he said.

"Good, because I'll probably forget. A lot."

Ugh. A lot sounded like *Lotty.* I had to start watching every word I said.

"I mean," I amended, "I might goof up and call you Teddy a whole *bunch* of times before I get used to Ted."

"Really, it's okay," he said, sniffling. "Maybe I'll start calling you *Ive* instead of Ivy."

"*I've*? Like *I've* got a broken leg?"

"Yeah," he said. "You've got a broken leg. And I've got a broken heart."

◇◇◇

What I learned from that:

Heartbreaks are contagious.
You can catch one from a phone call,
if it's your best friend calling with
the world's worst news.

◇◇◇

FOUR

◇◇◇

Room to Wonder

*T*eddy didn't want to come over the next few days, and I didn't blame him.

On Saturday morning, my dad was making his traditional weekend waffles. I was sitting at the kitchen table, feeling depressed.

"Let's take Winthrop to Forest Park," Dad said. "After breakfast. You, me, Mom, and Winthrop."

"Uh," I said. "No thanks."

I wanted to stay home in case Teddy called.

Neither of us had cell phones yet, so we were both tied to our landlines.

"We could pack a picnic," Dad said, checking on the waffles.

"That sounds fun," Mom called from the hallway. She was rearranging the gallery of framed photos. "We could ask someone in the park to take a family picture of us with Winthrop."

A terrible thought occurred to me as I looked at our dog, snoozing under the kitchen table.

"Why?" I said. "In case Winthrop *dies*?"

Mom stepped into the kitchen. "No," she said calmly. "Because I don't have any good family pictures of us with Winthrop."

"Yeah, right," I said.

I knew I sounded like a brat, but I was just so sad for Teddy. And because I didn't know how to be sad without crying, I was acting grumpy and mad. Mom had explained all this to me. She said we sometimes express one emotion (anger) when we're feeling something else (sadness).

"I don't feel like a picnic today," I said. "Sorry."

"You don't have to be sorry," Dad said, setting a plate of waffles in front me. "We can do whatever you'd like today."

I poured syrup over my waffles and watched the thick amber liquid disappear into the tiny squares.

"We could go to the art museum or to a movie," Dad said. "Or, hey, you know someplace I've always wanted to go? Scott Joplin's old house. It's a museum. We should check that out. Or the planetarium?"

"We could take an online masterclass," Mom called from the hallway. "Maybe pick up some new coding tricks?"

She was trying to make me laugh, but I couldn't. I couldn't feel happy when I knew Teddy was so sad. It would feel like a betrayal.

"Can we just hang out here today?" I said.

"That's good, too," Dad said. He was putting a plate of waffles at Mom's place at the table. "I have a million emails to answer." He called to Mom in the hallway. "Waffles, hon."

Mom joined me at the table. "Mmmm," she purred. "I'm heading over to Mr. Hobart's house at ten for coffee."

This was one of Mom's rituals. Every Saturday morning at ten o'clock, she had coffee with our neighbor across the street and three houses down. Mr. Hobart was by far the oldest person on Magnolia Circle and certainly the crabbiest, but Mom liked to visit him every week and make sure he was okay.

"After that," she said, "I might stop by the neighborhood meeting. People are gathering at the Morgans' house to organize an effort to stop the dead-end sign."

"What's up with that?" I asked, chewing.

"Well," said Mom, "I know Mr. Hobart has strong opinions about it. He told me last week he's convinced a sign that says *dead end* at the entrance to Magnolia Circle will bring down the value of all our houses. It could be a problem."

Dad turned from the stove and made a sour face. "I had a patient yesterday who needed quadruple bypass surgery. Twenty-nine years old and he has the heart of a ninety-five-year-old. *That's* a problem."

"Still, if we ever want to sell our house, a dead-end sign could be a problem," Mom said.

"Wait," I said. "We're going to sell our house? And *move*?"

"That's not what I'm saying," Mom said. "I'm saying if we ever *did* want to sell our house, we'd want to get the highest price for it. And if a sign that says *dead end* could hurt our chances of selling this house for the highest price, that would be a problem." She turned to Dad. "A first-world problem, yes, but a problem nonetheless."

"I'll be eager to hear what you find out at the neighborhood meeting," Dad said. He had joined us at the table with his plate and was drowning a stack of waffles in melted butter and syrup.

Mom raised her eyebrows while looking at Dad's plate. "Speaking of quadruple bypass surgery."

"It's my one indulgence," he said, dissecting his waffles into bite-size mouthfuls. He paused to pat his belly. "I promise I won't let it bring down my property value."

On Monday afternoon, I was sitting in a living room chair, facing Magnolia Circle, with my cast resting on an ottoman. I was rereading the first book in the Narnia series, with the phone in easy reach in case Teddy called.

Between chapters, I happened to look up and glance out the window. I saw Melvin Moss. He was the boy I was supposed to do my Trojan War project with, but he'd stopped coming to school. Nobody knew why.

I'd asked my teacher, Mrs. Seifert, about

Melvin, mainly because I wanted to know if he was going to help on the Trojan War project. She said she'd spoken with Melvin's mom.

"They move around a lot," Mrs. Seifert told me.

"Because of his parents' work?" I asked.

"I think it's more complicated than that," Mrs. Seifert said.

She seemed sad when she talked about Melvin, so I didn't ask her anything else. I knew Melvin wouldn't be back to help with "our" Trojan War project.

But there was Melvin now, across the street, in front of Teddy's brown-brick apartment building. Even from the window, I could tell it was Melvin by his hair. It was deep red, like the color of Lotty's fur.

Melvin was wearing a hoodie pulled up over

his head, so only the front of his scraggly hair was visible. I could see he looked shabby. His hoodie was stretched out and ripped. His jeans were too short—and not in a stylish way. He was holding a notebook.

I grabbed my crutches and hopped to the window. Melvin didn't see me because he was on the opposite side of the street. Now he was standing still and writing in his notebook. I had to smile, because Melvin was not exactly a good student. I'm guessing that's why Mrs. Seifert paired him with me. She probably knew I'd do most of the work on the Trojan War project and maybe I'd be a good influence on Melvin. (This is why I hated group projects.)

But now I was happy to see Melvin outside my window. I wanted to tell him we got a perfect score (100) on "our" Trojan War project.

If he was interested, I'd show him the Trojan horse I built using a shoebox, and the timeline of "Important Trojan War Events" I printed on a piece of yellow poster board.

I used one of my crutches to knock on the windowpane, hoping to catch Melvin's attention. He didn't hear it. So I used my knuckles to knock. I even yelled through the glass, "Melvin! Hey, Melvin! Hey!"

But the thermal glass was too thick. Or maybe Melvin was too far away. Whatever the reason, he didn't hear me.

Minutes later, a white van pulled up in front of Teddy's building. It looked like a delivery van. There were two windows for the driver and the passenger. The back of the van was paneled. Melvin climbed inside.

And then he was gone.

What I learned from that:

I should've hopped over and opened

the front door to say hey to Melvin,

but sometimes you don't think of the

right thing to do until it's too late.

FIVE

◇◇◇

Second Sighting

Seeing Melvin Moss gave me an excuse to call Teddy.

"You're not going to believe who I saw yesterday."

"Lotty?" Teddy asked.

I was trying to avoid the topic, but there it was.

"Not Lotty," I said. "Melvin Moss."

"Oh," said Teddy. "Is he still short?"

Teddy was the second-shortest boy in fourth grade. Melvin was the shortest. The two weren't close friends, mainly because they were in different homerooms. Teddy was in Mr. Frothingham's room. Melvin and I were in Mrs. Seifert's room. But Teddy knew Melvin. I think Teddy always appreciated that Melvin was shorter than him.

"Melvin looked the same," I said. "Only messier."

"Where'd you see him?" Teddy asked.

"He was standing in front of your building. I wonder if his family is moving into Magnolia Manor."

"We don't have any vacancies in our building. And I haven't heard anybody's moving out."

Teddy would know. He knew everyone who lived in the twenty-four apartments at Magnolia Manor.

"Anyway," I said, "I just thought you'd be interested. How are you, um, feeling?"

"Miserable," Teddy said.

I didn't want to mention Lotty, but I couldn't ignore it.

"Are you thinking about getting a new dog?" I asked.

"Too soon."

"I get it."

A beat of silence passed.

"How's Winthrop?" Teddy asked.

"Depressed," I said. "He misses Lotty. And you."

"Have you been taking him for his daily walk?"

"No. It's no fun without you."

Teddy sighed loudly. "I'll be over in ten minutes. If I cry, just ignore me."

I was getting better at using my crutches, but I still moved at a snail's pace. Teddy didn't seem to mind. As we made our way down our favorite path in Forest Park, I told him what I'd learned about the dead-end sign.

"My mom says they've collected enough signatures to convince the city *not* to put up the sign."

"My parents will be upset," Teddy said. "They're in favor of the sign."

"Because they think it'll mean more parking places on the street?" I asked.

"Yeah," he said. "The whole thing is ridiculous. How much power can one street sign have? And why do adults worry about *stupid* stuff, like street parking, when they could and *should* be solving canine leukemia?"

Teddy was doing the same thing I always did. He was feeling sad about Lotty but acting mad because it's easier to get mad than feel sad. I wasn't about to give him a lesson in emotional transference. I knew how annoying it was when Mom tried to teach me this stuff.

We walked for half an hour and then sat on a bench at the dog run for another thirty minutes while Winthrop ran around without a leash. As we were leaving the park, I saw a white van pulling out of Magnolia Circle.

"Look!" I said. "I think that's Melvin Moss."

"Where?" Teddy asked, turning around to look back at the park.

"No, *there*," I said, pointing at the white van driving away from us. "That's what Melvin was riding in yesterday. I think he really must be moving to our street."

"As long as he's still shorter than me," Teddy said. "I'll be furious if he's grown even one-eighth of an inch taller."

What I learned from that:

I'm not the only person who acts

mad when they feel sad.

SIX

◇◇◇

Turn It Around

The following week, I had an appointment with Dr. Ames. It had been three
weeks since my surgery. I had to get another
X-ray to see how my leg was healing under the
cast.

"Hello, hello," Dr. Ames said as he walked
into the examining room. He was holding the
X-ray in one hand and shaking Mom's hand
with the other.

"How's the leg look?" Mom asked.

"Well," Dr. Ames said, frowning, "the alignment's looking good, but I'm not seeing new callus formation. Not enough periosteal reaction." He turned to speak directly to me. "In plain English, that means the bones aren't healing as quickly as we'd like. I'm going to keep you in the long-leg cast for another three weeks."

I sighed heavily. I was sitting on the exam table, trying to balance the crutches with two fingers.

"What's your top speed on those things?" he asked.

"Zero miles per hour," I grumped.

"That's not true," Mom said. "She's doing quite well on them. The hardest part is getting up and down the front stairs at our house. But she's managing just fine. Right, Ivy?"

"I guess so," I said. "Mom and Dad help. And my best friend lives across the street. He helps me, too."

"Good, good, good," said Dr. Ames, nodding thoughtfully.

"But I can't go over to my friend's apartment because he lives on the fourth floor—no elevator."

"Mmmm," replied Dr. Ames. "I remember. Stairs are your enemy. But I'm glad you're mastering the art of walking with crutches. It's important to feel empowered and not like a victim."

He knocked on my cast for emphasis. I couldn't help but smile.

"So now, let's see," he said, reading from his

computer screen. "Last time we talked about the importance of having a project or a goal; something you might like to accomplish during your recovery journey. I'm curious to hear what you decided to do."

I'd totally forgotten about that conversation. It seemed like a lifetime ago.

"Um," I said. "I'm basically just trying to get better, y'know? Oh, and my best friend's dog died. So I'm trying to cheer him up about that."

Dr. Ames made his sad-clown face. "Right. Good. That's important. A dog and a best friend. Hmm."

He poked around my cast for a minute, asking if it felt too tight or too loose. It didn't.

"All right, then," he said. "Make the most of this journey, Ivy. Write down what you learn. I think you'll be surprised by the insights you can gain during difficult times."

On the drive home, Mom turned off the music to talk.

"You could be in a cast for two more months," she said. "Until the middle of August."

I sighed loudly. "School starts on August twenty-fourth. *Jeez*. The whole summer—wasted."

"Not necessarily," she said.

"How can you say that? This is the worst summer in the history of summers! First this stupid cast. Then Lotty. Then—"

"Turn it around, Ivy," Mom said, not taking her eyes off the road. "Turn it around."

It was one of Mom's favorite sayings. I bet her patients hated hearing it as much as I did.

"How can I *possibly* turn this terrible summer around?" I asked.

"You might consider taking Dr. Ames's advice," Mom said. "Make the most of your convalescence. Set a goal. Do something you care about. That's how you make it a good summer."

It was annoying how Mom made everything sound so easy and cute.

The mood in the car shifted when we turned down Magnolia Circle and saw two police cars parked in front of Teddy's apartment building. Another police car was arriving behind us. Its siren was blaring.

"What in the world?" Mom said, pulling into our driveway.

She helped me hobble up the stairs to our house. As soon as we were inside, I called Teddy.

"What's going on over there?" I asked, almost out of breath.

"Burglary on the third floor. Ms. Hiremath's unit."

"Oh no. What'd they take?"

"Jewelry, silverware, three hundred and fifty dollars in cash."

"Wow," I murmured, secretly delighted by the drama. "Any suspects?"

"No, and Joel feels terrible."

"Why does your doorman feel terrible?"

Teddy explained. "This morning around ten o'clock, some delivery guys came to Magnolia Manor with a new sofa. It was dark green. They said Ms. Hiremath ordered it. But she was at work, so the delivery guys asked Joel if he could let them into her apartment to drop off the sofa."

"Joel has a key to everyone's apartment, right?" I asked.

"Right," said Teddy. "So the guys delivered the sofa. Joel stayed with them the whole time."

"For security?"

"Exactly," said Teddy. "Then they went downstairs with Joel, and he called Ms. Hiremath to say her new sofa had arrived. The delivery guys were just about to leave when Joel said, 'Hold on a second. Ms. Hiremath says she didn't order a new sofa.'"

"She didn't?"

"No. So the guys went back upstairs. Joel unlocked the apartment and the delivery guys got the sofa. They carried it downstairs and left with it in their van. When Ms. Hiremath came home from work today, she discovered some valuable stuff was gone."

"Call the delivery guys," I said.

"They didn't leave a phone number. Or a business card."

"But surely they did it."

"Joel was with them the whole time," Teddy said.

"But . . . ," I started to say.

"But what?"

"I can see why Joel feels terrible."

"I *know*," said Teddy. "It wasn't his fault, but maybe it was a little? Who knows? I hope he doesn't quit. Do you think we should be nervous about living on a street where people are stealing stuff?"

"We have to solve this," I said quietly, like it was a prayer.

Teddy laughed. "You want to solve this crime?"

"No," I said. "I want *us* to solve this crime."

"Why?"

"Because," I replied calmly, "I need something to take my mind off this stupid cast, and you need something to take your mind off Lotty."

"And?" Teddy said.

"Solving a crime will accomplish both of those goals."

"I am never going to stop feeling sad about Lotty," Teddy said. "But you're right. It would be good to stop feeling sad every second of every day. Where do we start?"

"By deciding to start," I said with confidence.

I didn't even care that I sounded annoyingly like my mom.

What I learned from that:

It's important to feel empowered

so you don't feel like a victim.

◇◇◇

SEVEN

◇◇◇

Crime Wave

*T*eddy and I spent the next week turning my living room into a crime investigation unit.

We used poster board and playing cards to make a model of Magnolia Manor, all twenty-four units. We marked every entrance, every door and window, every way a burglar might get into the building while two sofa delivery guys distracted Joel. We also interviewed Ms. Hiremath.

"Do you have any theories on how the crooks got away with it?" I asked.

"No," Ms. Hiremath said. "But my insurance agent, Ben Kubicek, says he's heard of cases where thieves work in groups of three. One of the deliverymen could've distracted Joel while the other slipped into my bathroom, opened a window, and threw a rope ladder down for the real thief to enter."

Teddy's eyes brightened. "Even *I* could climb a rope ladder to your apartment."

Ms. Hiremath looked at Teddy sharply.

"But of course I didn't do it," said Teddy. "I'm not a thief."

"Of course you're not, Teddy," said Ms. Hiremath, softening.

"I go by *Ted* now. So in the future if you could remember to call me *Ted*, I'd be grateful. *Ted* sounds more grown-up than *Teddy*, don't you think?"

I needed to get the investigation back on track.

"Ms. Hiremath," I said, looking at my notes, "Joel said he stayed with the two men the whole time they were in your apartment."

"That's what he says," said Ms. Hiremath. "But when Ben, my insurance agent, asked Joel if either of the men used my restroom while they were here, Joel couldn't remember."

An hour later, we were back at my house, eating grilled peanut-butter-and-banana sandwiches.

"I think what we need to do," Teddy said, "is take a DNA sample of Ms. Hiremath's toilet." He paused to take an enormous bite of his sandwich. "Where can we get a DNA kit?"

"It's been almost a week since the burglary,"

I said. "I'm guessing Ms. Hiremath has cleaned her bathroom at least once."

I then suggested something I'd put off saying because it seemed unkind.

"You don't think Joel was involved, do you? Maybe he gets fifteen or twenty percent of the value of everything stolen, just for letting the burglars in and pretending to be oblivious to the crime?"

"No way, not Joel," said Teddy. "I mean, sure, it's *possible*. But he's been working in our building since before I was born. If he was going to steal stuff, wouldn't he have done it before now? Think of all the packages he could steal every December."

"You're right. I'll take Joel off the suspect list."

Unfortunately, he was the only name I'd had on my suspect list.

Teddy and I were drawing another poster of

Magnolia Manor, this time with all the fire escapes, when my dad came home from work.

"Better sharpen your pencils," Dad said as he walked in the front door. "Summer crime wave in St. Louis."

"What?" Teddy and I said at the same instant.

"Just heard it on the radio," Dad said. "Google it."

I hopped over to the kitchen laptop and typed in the search words: *Crime wave. Summer. St. Louis, Missouri.* An article from the *St. Louis Post-Dispatch* popped up immediately.

THIEVES POSING AS DELIVERYMEN DUPE DOORMAN, CUSTODIAN

◇◇◇

After two home burglaries in less than a week, authorities are warning St. Louis

residents to exercise caution when letting delivery people into apartment buildings.

"We don't want to frighten anyone, but this could be the beginning of a summer crime wave," said St. Louis Police Chief Sam MacPherson.

MacPherson explained how the scam works. "A team of deliverymen arrives at an apartment building with a sofa. They probably know in advance the victim won't be home."

In both cases, a building employee let the "deliverymen" into the victim's apartment with the sofa. The problem is, said MacPherson, the sofa is a ruse. The apartment dweller did not order a sofa. By the time the sofa is removed, less than an hour later, the thieves have also taken money and valuables from the apartment.

Karma Mathews was the victim of yesterday's burglary on Washington Avenue, which occurred in midafternoon, an unusual time for a home burglary.

"The thieves took all my fine jewelry,

including my grandmother's pearls," said Mathews. "My grandmother gave me that pearl necklace for my twenty-first birthday. How can I possibly replace it?"

Mathews says she is considering filing a lawsuit against the homeowners' association of her building, as well as the building's doorman, Daryl Steen.

"He let the fake delivery guys in without my permission," said Mathews. "And he didn't even stay with them the whole time. He called me from the lobby, while the thieves were upstairs, robbing me blind."

Daryl Steen refutes Mathews's account. "It's true I let the deliverymen in without Ms. Mathews's permission, but only because she didn't answer when I called her at work. So I let the men in with the sofa. I thought I was doing her a favor. But I never left their side. I was in the apartment with them the whole time. By the time Ms. Mathews finally called me back twenty minutes later, I was downstairs in the lobby with the guys. When Ms. Mathews told me she hadn't ordered a sofa, I returned to the apartment with the men and we got the sofa out of there."

Joel Shoemaker, custodian at Magnolia Manor on Magnolia Circle, said he never left the deliverymen alone in the apartment. That burglary also took place during the daytime while the occupant was at work.

Police Chief MacPherson asks anyone with information about two men, one Caucasian, one African American, reported to be in their late 20s or early 30s, seen delivering a green sofa from an unmarked white van with paneled sides to contact the St. Louis Police Department.

Teddy was shaking his head. "Joel is *not* going to be happy they called him a custodian. I mean, sure, that's officially what he is, but he's so much more than that. Everyone in the building relies on him to be there every morning and every night, just to say hey or help them—"

He stopped talking when he saw the expression on my face. "What's wrong?"

I spoke in a whisper. "Melvin Moss."

"What?" Teddy said.

I cleared my throat. "Remember how I saw Melvin getting in a white van in front of your house?"

Teddy scoffed. "The chances of this being the same white van are—"

"*Good*," I interrupted.

"You think Melvin Moss is a *thief*?"

"No," I said. "I mean, yes. I mean, I don't know. But something's up."

What I learned from that:

Sometimes the only thing you learn

is that you need to learn more.

EIGHT

◇◇◇

The Mastermind

O n Friday morning, Teddy and I were planning to walk Winthrop to Forest Park,
but we stopped on the way when we heard
Mr. Hobart yelling at us from his living room
window.

"*Two times*," Mr. Hobart hollered. He was
shaking the newspaper article at Teddy and
me. "They mention the burglary on Magnolia
Circle *two times!*"

I let Winthrop off the leash in Mr. Hobart's

front yard while Teddy helped me hop up the three steps to the house.

"Let yourself in," Mr. Hobart hollered from a living room chair. "I can't get up without my cane."

I'd always liked Mr. Hobart's house. It was a mix of gray stone and red brick with a pointy roof. The front door was rounded at the top and painted bright blue. It reminded me of a hobbit's house.

Mr. Hobart was still complaining when we joined him in his living room.

"It's worse than a dead-end sign," he said. "When people know we've had a burglary on Magnolia Circle, *no one* will want to live here."

"I still want to live here," said Teddy.

Mr. Hobart glared at Teddy. "Where's your dog? I haven't seen it lately."

Teddy closed his eyes. "*She* had canine leukemia. We had to put her down."

"Pfft!" Mr. Hobart said. "*That* old story. Well, let me tell you. There are worse things than dying."

As I looked at Mr. Hobart, I noticed he hadn't brushed his hair or shaved. That, combined with his grumpiness and storybook house, made him look like a forest troll. His living room was decorated with a beat-up old couch, two chairs, a coffee table, and a big, clunky television. My eyes drifted toward the dining room. A hospital bed, unmade, was parked awkwardly against one wall.

What's wrong with Mr. Hobart? I wondered. *If he's sleeping in a hospital bed, he must be sick.*

My thoughts were interrupted when Mr. Hobart grabbed his cane and began pointing out the window at Winthrop.

"He's making a tinkle in my yard!" Mr. Hobart yelled. "Look! Your stupid dog did it again! He made another tinkle in my yard. *Two* tinkles! He did it *two times*!"

"Suh-sorry," I stuttered. I grabbed my crutches with one hand and Teddy's neck with the other. "C'mon," I said. "Let's go."

Teddy couldn't shake off Mr. Hobart's words as we continued our walk to the park.

"Is there an award for the Meanest Man in America? Because I want to nominate Mr. Hobart. He'd win first place. He'd get a gold medal in the Mean Man Olympics."

"I don't think he realizes how mean he sounds," I said. "He's too unhappy to be nice."

I told Teddy about the hospital bed I'd seen in the dining room. "He must sleep downstairs. He probably can't get up the stairs to sleep in his bedroom."

"Then he should move to a one-story house," said Teddy. "On the other side of the city."

"Mr. Hobart will never leave Magnolia Circle," I said. "He's lived on our street forever. Besides, it'd be too hard for him to move all his stuff at his age."

"Then he should buy another house on—" Teddy started to say. He stopped walking and dropped his voice. "It's Mr. Hobart."

"What's Mr. Hobart?"

"Mr. Hobart is behind the burglaries," Teddy said. "The burglaries *and* the dead-end sign. Think about it: He's trying to lower the price of houses on our street so he can buy a *second* house on Magnolia Circle, a house that has only one story. That way, he can keep all his stuff in his current house and sleep in a bedroom on the first floor in another house."

"But there are no houses for sale on Magnolia Circle," I reminded Teddy.

"Pfft!" Teddy said, mimicking Mr. Hobart's dismissive sound. "He's trying to convince people on Magnolia Circle that it's not a safe place to live anymore. He's hoping to convince someone in a one-story house—and there are four of them on Magnolia Circle—to put their house up for sale. Then he'll buy it at a discount!"

"But he's the one who's against the dead-end sign," I said.

"It's a red herring!" Teddy cried.

"A what?'

"Red herring," Teddy repeated. "Didn't Mrs. Seifert teach you about red herrings?"

"No," I said. "Mrs. Seifert was completely obsessed with the Trojan War. It's all we studied last year."

"Mr. Frothingham was obsessed with mysteries," Teddy said. "It's his favorite genre. Every book he read us last year was a mystery. That's how I know about red herrings."

"They're a fish, right?"

"Literally, yes," said Teddy. "But a red herring is also a trick writers use to throw readers off the scent or to point them in the wrong direction."

"And?"

"Don't you get it? Mr. Hobart is trying to throw us off the trail!"

"You're not making sense, Teddy."

"My name is *Ted*."

"Okay, *Ted*, explain to me how Mr. Hobart could be behind a crime wave when he can't even walk up the stairs in his house. You really think he could carry a sofa in and out of a building?"

"I'm not saying Mr. Hobart is *literally* doing the heavy lifting. He's way too old for that."

"Exactly," I agreed. "So what are you saying?"

Teddy stopped and spoke in a slow, soft whisper. "What I'm saying is that Mr. Hobart is the mastermind. He's too sly to do the actual dirty work. He hires the two delivery guys."

"And he buys a sofa, too?" I asked.

"Why not? You can buy a cheap sofa for a couple hundred bucks. If he can lower the house prices on our street by even one or two percent, it's worth it! His house is probably worth five hundred thousand dollars."

I did the math in my head. One percent of five hundred thousand was five thousand dollars. Two percent was ten thousand dollars. Teddy was right. This was serious money.

Could Teddy's far-fetched theory possibly be true?

Just then, Winthrop barked and my cast started itching like the worst case of poison ivy. It seemed like the universe was sending me a sign—and it wasn't a dead-end sign. It was the opposite of a dead end, and it made me smile like the Cheshire Cat.

"I cannot believe," I said to Teddy, "that we have solved our very first crime."

◇◇◇

What I learned from that:

Crime solving is easy!

◇◇◇

NINE

◇◇◇

Hold the Ladder

When we got back from our walk, Teddy and I wrote up our theory about Mr. Hobart on a poster board. After we finished, we stood and admired our work.

"Now we have to catch him in the act," Teddy said.

"What?"

"We need proof," Teddy explained. "We need to see Mr. Hobart plotting his next crime.

Then we'll call the police and tell them we've solved the case. Can you climb a ladder?"

"*What?*"

"Never mind. You can hold the ladder. I'll climb it. There's a ladder in my building. If we set the ladder against Mr. Hobart's house, I'm sure we can see inside."

"Teddy, that's against the law."

"We're not going to *hurt* him. We just need proof that Mr. Hobart is the mastermind of the St. Louis summer crime wave."

"You might be right about him being the mastermind, but looking in his window is a terrible ide—"

"Ives, we are dealing with a man who can laugh over the death of an innocent dog. Do you really think we have time to waste?"

I tried to explain that Mr. Hobart didn't

exactly *laugh* about poor Lotty's death, but Teddy was barreling ahead.

"We'll do it tomorrow morning," he said. "After breakfast. I'll carry the ladder over to his house and set it up in the bushes, next to his window. Then I'll come back here and help you down the stairs."

"And what'll I do?"

"You just have to hold the ladder for me. I don't want to break my leg, too. No offense."

"But—" I tried to say.

"And leave Winthrop at home. We can't have any barking. We don't want Mr. Hobart to know we're wise to his diabolical ways."

The next morning, after forcing down a waffle, I waited for Teddy on my front porch. I was already nervous about this mission. Teddy was sweating when he arrived.

"I should've brought a camera," he said. Then he waved away the thought. "Oh, well. The police will just have to believe me when I tell them what I saw."

Teddy helped me down the front steps of my house.

"What do you think you're going to see?" I asked.

"I'm guessing he probably has a map of the city with pushpins stuck in places he wants to rob next. Maybe a pile of stolen cash and jewelry, too."

"I didn't see a map when we were there yesterday," I said. "Or cash. Or jewelry."

"He's not going to leave the loot in *plain*

sight," Teddy said. "That's why we have to watch him when he doesn't know we're watching him. See the ladder?"

A metal ladder was hidden in a tangle of scratchy bushes next to a side window of Mr. Hobart's house.

"If you can just hold the ladder steady for me," Teddy whispered as he forced his way through the bushes.

I could tell he was nervous, because his legs were shaking as he stepped on the first rung of the ladder.

"Make sure you're holding it tight," he whispered over his shoulder.

"I am," I whispered back.

"Really tight."

"I *am*."

I listened to the muffled sounds of Mr. Hobart's TV while Teddy climbed five rungs of the ladder. His face was now level with the bottom of the window.

"Is he there?" I said quietly. "Can you see him?"

"Yeah, he's there. Sitting in a chair."

"What's he doing?"

"Just sitting."

"Do you see anything that looks . . . stolen?"

"Not yet."

"Can he see you?"

"No. Not unless he turns his head."

The palms of my hands were sweating from the combination of heat and stress. I started to reposition my hands but momentarily lost my grip on the ladder, causing it to slip an inch.

"Ivy!" Teddy hissed.

"Sorry! My hands slipped!"

Teddy readjusted his footing. He was breathing heavily.

"What's he doing now?" I whispered.

"Just sitting. Looking out the window. Wait a sec."

"What?"

"Someone's at the front door."

"Oh no."

"Someone's knocking, but Mr. Hobart's not getting up to answer it."

"Oh no."

"The door's opening. This could be his partner in crime! This is it, Ives!"

But I knew it wasn't it. I knew the person at the door was no partner in crime.

"Is it my mom?" I whispered.

"Yeah," Teddy whispered back. "How'd you know?"

Because it was Saturday morning at ten o'clock. She was there for their weekly coffee date. How had I forgotten this?

"Do *not* let my mom see you," I said. "Teddy, whatever you do, do *not* let her see you. Get *down*. Now! Quietly. Please!"

"Okay. I'm coming right dow—"

That's when Teddy's forehead hit the window, causing a loud *thwunk*. Even I heard what Mom said next.

"Mr. Hobart, I apologize for the interruption," she said in her calm but stern voice. "I'll be back in thirty minutes. Ivy and Teddy, come with me."

Turns out our neighbor, Mr. Hobart, suffered from agoraphobia, which is a mental condition that makes it nearly impossible for people to leave their homes. Mom was Mr. Hobart's psychiatrist. That's why she went to his house every Saturday morning at ten o'clock. It was their weekly appointment.

Mom sent Teddy back to his building with the ladder. Then she sat me down in our living room for a talk.

"The poor man hasn't left his house in three years," Mom said. "*Three years*, Ivy. He's a lonely old man with mental health issues. And you're *spying* on him?"

"I'm sorry," I mumbled.

"*Excuse me?*" Mom said.

"I said I'm sorry. I jumped to conclusions."

"I'm glad we agree on that," Mom said. She

took a deep breath. "Do you think what you did was fair to Mr. Hobart? Or kind?"

"No," I mumbled.

"*Excuse me?*" Mom said.

"No," I said again, louder. "It wasn't fair or kind. But the ladder wasn't even my idea. I knew it was wrong. I just—"

"I don't care *whose* idea it was. You *knew* it was a bad idea, and you participated. I want you to write a letter of apology."

"He didn't even *see* us!"

"It doesn't matter," Mom said flatly. "I want you to write it anyway. Apologies are important."

She reached into a desk drawer and pulled out a clean sheet of paper.

"Here," she said. "There are pens in every room of the house. Write the letter. I'll deliver it when I see him next Saturday."

"What am I supposed to write?"

"Acknowledge your mistake, say you're sorry, and commit in a meaningful way to doing better in the future."

I spent the next hour staring at the blank page. Finally, I wrote the letter.

Dear Mr. Hobart,

This morning I violated your privacy.

I mistakenly thought you were the

mastermind of a criminal operation, but

I was the one who was up to no good.

I'm very sorry for what I did. I will try

my best to make it up to you. I thought

about giving you my birthday money ($55),

but my mom told me "monetary restitution

is not appropriate in this situation." So I'll

try to find another way to be a good neighbor to you. Maybe we can even become friends.

Sincerely sorry and determined to do better,

Ivy Crowden

<hr />

Later that night, when I realized Mom was too mad to eat and Dad was engrossed in a book, I slunk into the kitchen and made a sandwich with two heels of raisin bread and a glop of peanut butter. I ate it in my bedroom. The sandwich sat like a rock in my stomach.

"*Primum non nocere*," Dad said. He was standing in the doorway to my bedroom, his book tucked under his arm.

"What?" I replied.

"It's Latin for 'First, do no harm.' It's part of

the Hippocratic oath doctors take. It's not a bad motto for life, Ivy. Above all else, we must try to do no harm to people."

"I know," I said.

"I know you know," Dad said.

An hour later, Mom stopped by my room. "Lights out," she said. "Time for bed."

I nodded and reached for my bedside lamp. Mom came over to my bed and kissed me softly on my head.

"Tomorrow's another day," she whispered in the dark. "Turn it around."

What I learned from that:

Never go along with an idea

you know is a mistake.

TEN

◇◇◇

Finally, a Phone

Winthrop had been moping around without Lotty. My dog hated fireworks, so Teddy and I decided to spend the Fourth of July at my house. We kept Winthrop's ears covered while we struggled to assemble a maddening five hundred–piece puzzle of a Monet haystack.

The following Friday, I had my six-week appointment with Dr. Ames. A cast technician used a saw to remove my fiberglass cast. I must've looked scared, because he did his best to reassure me.

"Don't worry," he said. "I won't cut your leg. The saw blade vibrates back and forth. It's the vibration that severs the cast."

Once my cast was off, I had another round of X-rays. Then Mom and I waited in an examining room for Dr. Ames. I couldn't take my eyes off my leg. It looked so shriveled up and skinny.

Dr. Ames knocked on the door three times to announce his arrival. "How are we feeling?"

"Same," I replied.

"Well, your leg isn't the same," he said happily, looking at my X-ray.

"It's not?"

"No. It's looking significantly better. You're healing nicely. There's no need to put you back in a long-leg cast."

"Seriously?" My heart did a backflip.

"Seriously," Dr. Ames said. "I'm going to put you in a short-leg cast."

My heart belly flopped. "Oh. I thought you meant we were done."

"We're about halfway done. We'll get you in a short-leg cast today that will reach just below your knee."

"Whatever. I'll still have to use crutches."

Dr. Ames stroked his chin. "We could try a scooter."

"A scooter?" I repeated. "Cool."

"It might not be the kind of scooter you're thinking of," Dr. Ames said. "This is a knee scooter."

He showed me a picture on his phone of a contraption that had four wheels, a padded seat to rest my knee on, handlebars, and a basket with a cupholder. It looked like a cross between a regular scooter, a bike, and a grocery cart.

Mom looked at the picture, too. "Is that better than crutches?"

"It's an alternative to crutches," Dr. Ames said. "Ivy, I want you to start putting some weight on your leg when you're at home. You've healed enough to start walking without crutches. Use the knee scooter when you're out and about to keep from getting tired or reinjuring your leg. The scooter will be a nice tool for our final phase of this journey."

I rolled my eyes at the word *journey*, but not enough for Mom to get mad. I was just so tired of the whole ordeal. My entire summer was going to be ruined by one stupid fall down the front stairs of our house.

At least the short cast was not as heavy as the

long cast. And I had to admit, the knee scooter would be more fun than crutches.

Teddy's tenth birthday was the following Thursday. To celebrate, his parents took him, his sister, Daphne, and me to Six Flags in nearby Eureka. To my surprise, I didn't have to skip any of the rides because of my cast, not even the American Thunder roller coaster.

On the way home, we stopped for frozen custard. It's what Teddy wanted instead of a birthday cake. He opened his presents while we sat outside.

I gave him *The Collected Stories of Sherlock Holmes.* "Hope you don't mind that I read it first," I said.

"Are you kidding?" Teddy said. "I love a pre-read book. And I love mysteries. Thanks, Ives."

His parents gave him a pizza box from Chicago Pizza. Inside was a gift certificate for a stand-up comedy workshop at Second City in Chicago.

"Oh, wow, thanks so much," Teddy said, hugging his mom and then his dad. "You guys know I've been wanting to try stand-up forever."

Daphne gave Teddy his last gift, which was by far the best gift. It was her old cell phone.

"It's nothing fancy," Daphne said as Teddy unwrapped it. "But at least it's a phone. You'll be on the family plan."

"Finally!" Teddy cried, holding the phone over his head "My life can begin! Thank you, thank you, thank you!"

I tried to smile, but I'm sure it looked fake. My parents weren't planning to get me a phone until I turned twelve.

"Don't worry, Ives," Teddy said. "We can get by with one phone between us, at least until school starts."

Teddy and I fully expected to be in different homerooms for fifth grade. We'd been in the same homeroom only once, back in first grade. Teachers thought it was a good idea to split up best friends. It never made sense to me.

The next night, Teddy and I walked with my knee scooter to Forest Park to watch an outdoor production of *Annie*.

The seats were free, but the July night was so hot and muggy, we left at intermission. On the way home, Teddy was singing "It's the Hard-Knock Life."

That's when I saw it.

"Teddy, look!" I said, pointing.

"It's *Ted*," he said, continuing to sing.

"Be quiet and *look*. Do you see it?" I was pointing at the bumper-to-bumper traffic on Skinker Boulevard.

"See what?" Teddy said.

"The white van! Right there! Look who's climbing into the passenger seat. Isn't that Melvin Moss?"

I was sure it was him. Melvin was wearing a baseball cap. His red hair was peeking out from underneath.

"I'm not sure," Teddy said tentatively. "Maybe?"

"It's *him*," I said. "I'm positive. One hundred percent positive. Did Daphne have the DriveMeThere app on her old phone?"

"I think so," said Teddy, looking at the birthday present from his sister. "Mom and Dad said she could use it in case of emergency."

"*This* is an emergency. Open the DriveMe-There app. We need a ride now!"

"Wow!" Teddy said, fumbling with his new phone. "This is going to be so much better than *Annie!*"

◇◇◇

What I learned from that:

The best drama always takes

place offstage.

◇◇◇

ELEVEN

◇◇◇

Run! Scoot! Drive!

I t took us a minute or two to figure out how the DriveMeThere app worked.

"There!" Teddy finally said, looking at his phone. "I think I did it."

"Let me see."

I'd watched my mom and dad use Drive-MeThere. I knew what to look for. "It says our driver is Maureen. She's in a blue Honda Civic. The plate number is listed here. She'll arrive in one minute."

"How's that possible with all this traffic?" Teddy asked. "Nobody's moving."

Just then a blue car flashed its lights. It was a Honda Civic with Maureen's license plate.

"That's her, Teddy! That our ride. C'mon. Run!"

"I'm running," he said. "Scoot!"

"I'm scooting!" I said, pushing my knee scooter as fast as I could.

Teddy opened the car door while I poked my head in to speak with the driver.

"Maureen?" I said.

"Yep," she said. "Daphne?"

"Close enough," I answered.

"I'm not supposed to pick up unaccompanied minors," Maureen said. "But I can see you're in a bit of a pickle with that cast on your leg."

"We're on serious business," Teddy said.

"There's a white van ahead of us," I said. "Can you follow it?"

"I can try," Maureen said. "You set your destination as the Gateway Arch."

"Never mind that," I said. "Just follow the white van. A redheaded boy is sitting in the front passenger seat."

"I'll do my best," Maureen said.

I folded my knee scooter and threw it in the backseat. We were off.

Maureen drove us down Skinker Boulevard to Lindell. Traffic was still bad. She turned on Lindell. I watched as we passed the Missouri History Museum on our right and then the Chase Park Plaza Hotel on our left.

"I think I see your van ahead of us," Maureen said.

"Good!" I said. "Keep your eye on it. Please."

Lindell Boulevard turned into Olive Street. Teddy was staring out his side of the car. "When you guys see the street sign for Olive, do you read it as *olive*, like the garnish, or *oh-live*, like the command?"

"Teddy, c'mon," I said. "Eyes on the prize. We're trying not to lose the white van."

"Wait, there it is!" he said. "It just turned left! See it, Maureen?"

"I do," she said.

"Drive fast!" I said. "Please! We have to see where this van is going."

Five minutes later, we were on Delmar Boulevard. Maureen pulled over.

"Sorry," she said, "but I lost the van a couple of lights back. It might've turned on Jefferson, but I'm not sure."

"It's okay," I said. "We'll get out here."

Maureen pointed at a tall brick house across the street.

"Have you guys ever been there?" she asked. "It's where Scott Joplin once lived. You know, the famous piano composer? The so-called 'king' of ragtime music?"

"Huh," I said, barely listening. Another person trying to get me interested in the Scott Joplin house when all I cared about was finding Melvin Moss and the mysterious white van.

"How much do we owe you?" Teddy asked.

Maureen turned around from the front seat and grinned. "This is your first DriveMeThere ride, isn't it? I thought so. You guys don't owe me anything. It's billed to the credit card linked to this account."

"Great," Teddy said.

"Thanks," I added.

After Maureen helped unload my knee scooter, Teddy and I stood on Delmar Boulevard. We waved as she drove away. It was pitch-dark. For the first time all night I felt scared.

We wandered on foot and scooter for almost an hour. We must've been walking in circles, because we found ourselves in front of Scott Joplin's old house again.

"It's a museum," Teddy said. "Look at the sign. It's part of the Missouri State Park system. How can a house be a park?"

I started to answer but was interrupted by the sound of Teddy's phone chirping. He answered on the third chirp.

"Hey, Mom," he said, looking at me with a face that said, *uh-oh*. "Yeah, *Annie* was good.

Kinda cheesy, but good. Where are we? Almost home. We're a bit late because . . ."

He was looking at me again. I shrugged. Then I pointed to my knee scooter and mouthed the words: *Flat tire?*

"Ivy's scooter got a . . . flat tire," Teddy said.

He was still talking to his mom while staring at me with wide-open eyes, like, *Is that the best you can do?*

"I know," he said. "Weird, right? Yeah. Okay. Sorry, Mom. We'll be home soon."

He ended the call.

"Flat tire?" he said, making a face.

"I couldn't think of anything better."

"We've got to get home before my mom gets really worried."

He took a step into the street and looked in both directions. "Think Maureen's still around?"

"We can try to get her," I said. "Open the DriveMeThere app and request a ride back to your house."

Ten minutes later, our driver, Oakes, arrived. He wasn't as chatty as Maureen, and he drove a lot faster. But not so fast that I didn't see it: the white van with paneled sides. It was parked in front of a place called Victory Mission, not three blocks from Scott Joplin's house.

This time I didn't jump to conclusions. I needed more information. But at least I knew what the next step should be.

What I learned from that:

Taking small, logical steps

isn't nearly as fun as jumping

to conclusions. But it feels

more professional.

TWELVE

⟡

Scott Joplin's House

T he next day was Saturday. Dad was making omelets for a change.

"Hey," I said, trying to sound as casual as possible as I waited for my breakfast, "can we go to the Scott Joplin museum today? And can Teddy come with us?"

Dad nearly dropped the omelet pan.

"I would *love* to do that," he said. "And of course Teddy can come along."

Mom was pouring milk into her coffee. "I'll

have to pass. Mr. Hobart and I have a two-hour session scheduled today."

I didn't say anything. I knew she was still mad at me for spying on Mr. Hobart.

"Call Teddy and tell him we'll leave around eleven," said Dad. "We can grab lunch down-town, after the museum."

At a quarter to twelve, Dad was getting frustrated.

"Where the devil is this place?" he asked. "I must've driven past it a million times over the years. Why can't I find it now?"

"The address is 2658 Delmar Boulevard," I said.

The number was seared into my memory

from the night before, but I couldn't tell my dad that.

"I, um, looked it up online," I fibbed.

"Good for you, Ivy," Dad said. "I'm impressed."

Teddy had to put his hand over his mouth to keep from laughing.

"There!" Dad said. "It's that red-brick building."

We were just in time to catch the noon tour. Our guide, Liam, began by telling us some background information about Scott Joplin, the King of Ragtime.

"We're not exactly sure what year he was born," Liam explained. "It was either 1867 or 1868, after the Civil War. So, unlike his father, Scott Joplin was born a free African American man, but he still faced the challenges of the day. His father abandoned the family. His mother cleaned homes for wealthy white people for free if they'd let young Scott practice on their pianos."

We learned that Scott Joplin lived in this house for less than two years.

"It wasn't a long time," Liam said, "but it was an important time for Joplin. While living here, he worked on some of his best 'rags,' including, we think, 'The Entertainer.'"

"What makes a song a 'rag'?" I asked.

"Good question," said Liam. "*Rag* is short for 'ragged' playing, but there's an undeniable structure to it. Think of it as a cross between European classical music and African American folk music. Ragtime is meant to sound loose and free, as if the pianist were just doodling around on the keys."

Liam used the foot pedals on a player piano

to move a paper roll through the piano. Every hole on the paper roll represented a note on the piano. In some places, the music sounded upbeat and jaunty. Other times it sounded sad, like someone's heart was breaking.

"This piece is called 'Solace,'" Liam said. "Listen to the melancholy undertones. Much of Joplin's music is bittersweet. A little bit happy and a little bit sad."

I thought about Melvin Moss. *Bittersweet* was exactly the right word to describe him. There was always something a little bit sad about Melvin, even though he put on a happy face.

"Joplin often included instructions on his musical compositions," Liam explained. "He wrote things like, 'Do not play this piece fast.' He wanted his music to be heard and more importantly, *felt*."

Dad, Teddy, and I were the only people on the tour. We moved from room to room, listening to Liam's stories and anecdotes about Scott Joplin and his famous piano music.

"When Joplin lived here," said Liam, "there was no indoor plumbing."

Teddy's arm shot up in the air, a habit from school. "So how did he—"

"Chamber pots," said Liam. "And an outhouse in the backyard."

Dad was admiring one of the pianos in the upstairs' sitting room. "So I'm guessing Joplin played in clubs around St. Louis while he lived here?"

"That's right," said Liam. "He played in bars and bawdy saloons."

"Sounds like a fun life," Dad said wistfully.

"Maybe," said Liam. "But when he died in 1917, John Stark, who was Joplin's music publisher, wrote: 'Scott Joplin is dead. A homeless itinerant, he left his mark on American music.'"

"Hold on," Teddy said. "Scott Joplin was *homeless?*"

Liam nodded. "Maybe not homeless in the way we think of it today. He had a place to live, usually a room or two he rented in a boarding house. But he moved around a lot."

Wait. That was exactly how Mrs. Seifert had described Melvin Moss. *They move around a lot.*

Liam was still talking. "When John Stark called Joplin *homeless*, he didn't mean he lived in Victory Mission."

I felt goose bumps on my arms.

"Victory Mission," I repeated. "What it that, anyway?"

"Victory Mission is the largest homeless shelter in St. Louis," Liam said. "You'll see the line for the soup kitchen when you leave, if you drive down Jefferson."

❧

After the tour, Dad couldn't stop talking about how inspired he was to get a piano for our house.

"It's something I've always wanted to do," he said dreamily as we walked to the car. "Play the piano. Maybe we could find a piano teacher who'd be willing to come to the house and give you, me, and Mom lessons. Teddy, you'd be welcome to take lessons at our house, too, if you're interested. I'd love to be able to play some old ragtime tunes. Or what about classical music? Think it's too late for this old dog to learn some new tricks?"

"No way," said Teddy. "I bet you could play some cool stuff with just a few lessons."

"You think so, Ivy?" Dad asked.

"Uh-huh," I said distractedly.

I wasn't thinking about a piano or lessons. All I could think about was Victory Mission and whether Melvin Moss might be living there. That would explain why he looked so scruffy.

"Shall we grab some lunch?" Dad asked. "Pizza, anyone?"

"Pizza sounds great to me," Teddy said. "Ives?"

"Yeah, sure, pizza," I said. "Hey, Dad, on the way to lunch, can you drive down Jefferson? I want to see Victory Mission."

Liam was right. The line for the soup kitchen was almost a block long. The white delivery van was still parked across the street. *Was Melvin Moss living there?*

Later that afternoon Teddy and I were sitting on my front steps when I asked the question that had been ricocheting around in my head all day long: "Do you think Melvin Moss might be homeless?"

"I guess. It's possible."

"Then why he is riding around in a white delivery van?"

"I'm not sure he is," said Teddy. "Remember, I've never seen him."

But I had. I *knew* I'd seen Melvin Moss in that van.

It occurred to me that Teddy might not even remember what Melvin looked like. They were never in the same class together like Melvin and I were.

"If his family has a van, wouldn't they rather live in it instead of at a homeless shelter?" I asked. "They could park the van in Forest Park and camp out. It'd be safer than living in a homeless shelter."

"What's so dangerous about homeless shelters?" Teddy said.

"I'm not sure, but I think they can be scary. People don't go there unless they're desperate. Desperate people do desperate things, like steal."

I knew this because some of my mom's patients had been homeless for months, sometimes years. Mom never told me their names, but she told me stories. She said when I was in high school, we could volunteer at a homeless shelter, serving meals or reading to the kids.

"We have to go back," I told Teddy.

"Where?" he said.

"Victory Mission. We have to find out if Melvin Moss is living there."

"And if he is?" Teddy said.

"I don't know. Let's take this investigation one step at a time."

Teddy smiled. "Or like Scott Joplin said about his piano compositions: 'Do not play this piece fast.'"

Just then Dad burst out the front door.

"I did it!" he said. "It's coming!"

"Huh?" I said. "What's coming?"

"Our piano!" Dad sang. "I just ordered it. It'll be here in a month."

What I learned from that:

Dad really wanted a piano.

THIRTEEN

◇◇◇

Are You Looking for Me?

The next morning, Teddy and I met in front of my house.

"My mom's home," he said. "We better not call DriveMeThere until we get a few blocks away."

So we requested one when we got to Skinker Boulevard. Our driver's name was Kevin.

"Victory Mission?" he asked when we opened the car door.

"That's right," said Teddy. "It's on Jefferson."

It took us less than ten minutes to get there.

When we entered the lobby, we saw a woman sitting behind a desk. She was busy and didn't look up from her paperwork.

"Excuse me," I said. "Is there someone named Melvin Moss living here?"

"We're not authorized to share the names of guests," she replied automatically, still looking down.

"But Melvin is a friend of ours," I explained.

"We're worried about him," Teddy added.

The woman finally lifted her eyes. She spoke without emotion. "It would be a violation of privacy to disclose the name of any of our guests, past or present."

I looked at Teddy. His face registered the same sense of defeat I was feeling. We were almost to the door when we heard him.

"Are you looking for me?"

It was a small, soft voice. I turned around. There he was. Melvin Moss!

He was wearing a baseball cap. He had a tool belt around his waist.

At first I was too stunned to speak. Finally, I said, "Melvin?"

And then, because I hadn't planned what I'd say when, or if, I saw him, I just said the first thing that popped into my head. "We got a hundred on our Trojan War project!"

Melvin smiled. I was guessing he probably felt guilty for not helping me with the project. I didn't have the heart to tell him I hadn't been expecting much help from him. He was never the smartest kid in the class. That's what I'd thought, anyway.

Turns out I was wrong. Melvin Moss *was* smart. He knew more about the Trojan War than I did. He explained it all to Teddy and me as we sat at a picnic bench behind Victory Mission.

Melvin's father was "out of the picture," he said. His mother was in a rehab clinic.

"Drugs," he said quietly.

"So you're here all alone?" Teddy said.

"If you mean without my parents, yeah," Melvin said. "But look around. I'm hardly alone."

I looked at a cluster of men leaning against the brick building. Most were smoking cigarettes. A little girl, maybe four years old, was riding a too-small tricycle in a raggedy patch of grass in front of them.

In some ways, Melvin seemed completely out of place at Victory Mission. He was a kid like me. He was someone I knew. *How could my classmate, my Trojan War partner, live in a homeless shelter?*

In other ways, Melvin Moss seemed to fit right in. His eyes looked tired, like those of the men who were smoking. He smelled like a wet basement. His face was dirty. Little red bumps dotted his forehead. *Were those bug bites? Acne?*

"Shouldn't you be with a foster family or something?" Teddy asked.

"I was," Melvin replied. "But I hated it there, so I ran away."

Poor Melvin. It must've been awful for him. I couldn't think of anything helpful to say.

"So, you're here," I said, stating the obvious.

"Did you know I'm pretty handy?" Melvin asked, changing the subject. "I've been fixing stuff around here. Just little things. I like to earn my keep."

I asked Melvin if he knew anything about the burglary at Ms. Hiremath's apartment and the similar crime on Washington Avenue.

Melvin snapped. "Why would I know anything about that?" he said hotly, standing up from the picnic bench.

"I thought I saw you in a white van in our neighborhood. That's all."

"So what if I was?" He was shifting his weight from one foot to the other. He wouldn't look at me.

Melvin was getting defensive, I could tell. He was like the raccoon I once saw in our backyard, rummaging through the garbage. When I turned on the porch light, the raccoon froze, jazz hands up, and stared at me as if to say: *Am I in trouble? Who, me?*

"You're not in trouble," I told Melvin. "But there's a crime wave in St. Louis. There seems to be a pattern to the robberies involving two guys in a white van delivering a sofa. I thought you might know something about them."

Melvin took off the baseball cap. His greasy hair fell in front of his eyes. "I know everything about them," he said.

"Will you tell us?" I asked.

"We're not just being nosy," Teddy added. "We want to help."

Melvin didn't answer. The silence hovered in the air above us. He was still standing, his eyes focused on something vague and far away. Then he covered his eyes with the heels of his hands. I wondered if he was going to cry.

"If you don't want to talk about it, you don't have to," I said. "But sometimes talking helps."

I was shocked to hear myself say something Mom might say, but I knew it was true.

Melvin folded his legs under the picnic bench and dropped his elbows on the table. He told us about two men who had approached him at Victory Mission.

"It was right after I got here," he began, almost in a whisper. "In the middle of May, these two guys said they'd call the authorities and have me sent back to foster care if I didn't help them pull off a burglary. They wanted me to drive their van while they robbed a bank. They said they could teach a smart kid like me to drive in one day."

"*What?*" I gasped.

"Don't worry," Melvin said. "I didn't do it. I

knew robbing a bank was a terrible idea. We would've been caught for sure. Banks have cameras everywhere."

"But you did something else?" Teddy asked.

"Yeah," said Melvin. "And it was my idea."

Melvin told us he'd been thinking about the Trojan War, and how the Greeks had built an enormous hollow wooden horse.

"Remember?" Melvin said, looking at me.

"Yes," I replied, remembering the Trojan horse I'd built out of a shoebox. "But Teddy wasn't in Mrs. Seifert's class. They didn't study the Trojan War. You have to tell him what happened."

"Well," Melvin said, turning to Teddy, "the Greeks built this huge wooden horse. Then they hid their best warriors inside it. They pretended the horse was a gift for the people of Troy. When the Trojans saw the horse, they thought it meant the Greeks were surrendering. So they dragged the heavy horse inside the city gates."

"But it was a trick," I said, picking up the story. "After the people of Troy went to sleep, the Greek soldiers climbed out of the horse. They opened the gates of the city so the rest of the Greek army could enter Troy."

"And that was the end of Troy," Melvin said.

Teddy looked confused. "What does any of this have to do with the crime wave sweeping St. Louis?"

"I'll tell you," said Melvin. "There was a new sofa here at Victory Mission. I asked the two guys to get me some plywood and a circular saw. I built a secret compartment inside it. It was big enough that I could lie flat in it."

"Inside the sofa?" I asked.

"Yeah," said Melvin. "The sofa was my Trojan horse. I hid inside it. The guys delivered the sofa to apartment buildings where we knew people would be at work during the day."

"How'd you know when they'd be gone?" I said.

"Most people keep the same work schedule from week to week," Melvin explained.

"That's why you were in our neighborhood," I said. "Making notes about people's schedules."

"Yeah," said Melvin, using his finger to draw invisible patterns on the picnic table.

"So the guys delivered the sofa," I said, trying to piece together Melvin's story with what I'd read in the newspaper. "Was it green?"

"Yeah," said Melvin. "How'd you know that?"

"Just keep going," I said.

"Okay," said Melvin. "So the guys put the sofa

in the apartment and left. That's when I crawled out of my secret compartment and looked for valuable things to steal. I knew I didn't have a lot of time, so I went for the easy stuff. Jewelry, money, that kind of thing."

Teddy was shaking his head. "How did you know how to build a secret compartment inside a sofa?"

Melvin grinned. "That was the fun part. I like making things with my hands."

I took a deep breath. "Melvin, you have to tell someone."

"No way. They'll send me to another foster home."

"What if I told Mrs. Seifert?" I said.

"You want to tell our *teacher*? She'll make me repeat fourth grade."

"Not necessarily," I said. "Mrs. Seifert was

really worried about you. I bet we can find her phone number or email address."

"We can definitely find it," said Teddy.

Melvin laid his cheek down on the picnic table as if he was too exhausted to hold up his head. "If the two guys find out I told . . . ," he murmured in a wounded voice, as if already dreading the punishment.

"The police will protect you from the thieves," I said. "Mrs. Seifert will know how to handle it. You have a good explanation."

He lifted his head off the bench. "Maybe we should tell Mrs. Seifert." Then his face brightened. "I want to tell her about the Trojan sofa I built. She'll like that part!"

Teddy was tapping away on his phone. "I'm on the school website. There's a staff directory with all the teachers' email addresses. Should I email Mrs. Seifert? Will she check her school email during the summer?"

"Yes," I said. "She's teaching summer school. Email her."

"What should I write?" Teddy asked, his nose up against his phone.

"Ask her to please call me on your phone," I said. "Say Ivy Crowden and Melvin Moss need to talk to her about their Trojan War project."

What I learned from that:

Maybe we're all Trojan horses

with secrets hidden inside of us,

and we have no idea how heavy

other people's secrets are.

FOURTEEN

✦✦✦

A Week Without Teddy

*T*eddy and I knew we couldn't tell our parents about Melvin Moss—not until we were sure Melvin wouldn't get in trouble.

Besides, Teddy was in enough trouble already. When his mom and dad found out Teddy had been billing our DriveMeThere rides to their credit card, Teddy lost cell phone privileges for a week. He probably would've been grounded, too, but his family was leaving for their annual Michigan vacation.

One week without Teddy, right when our investigation was heating up. The timing couldn't have been worse.

I couldn't even call Melvin because the last time I'd talked with Mrs. Seifert, she said Melvin was advised by his lawyer (Mrs. Seifert's husband) not to talk to anyone until he'd spoken with the police. Melvin was staying with the Seiferts while Mr. Seifert helped Melvin get right with the law.

The only friend I had left was Winthrop. So the day after Teddy left for Michigan, I shampooed Winthrop with our garden hose, careful to keep my cast dry. Then I dug out my dog brush and gave Winthrop a full-body brushing.

"C'mon, boy," I said. "Let's go to Forest Park. Just the two of us."

Winthrop looked at me like he'd been waiting to hear those words his whole life.

I scooter-walked Winthrop to the dog run in the center of Forest Park, let him off his leash, and parked my scooter. Winthrop's clean, floppy bangs flew back as he ran, smiling, to play with the other dogs. I knew he'd be covered in dirt within five minutes, but he looked so happy I didn't care.

I sat on a bench and stared at the frolicking dogs. I was still thinking about Melvin Moss and all the people who lived at Victory Mission. Were they allowed to bring their pets to the shelter, and if not, what happened to homeless animals?

That's when I saw her: the dog who looked exactly like Lotty. She was with a girl about my age. I stood up from my bench and walked with my scooter the fifty yards or so over to the girl with the Lotty look-alike.

"Hey!" I said. "What a sweet dog."

The girl looked at me strangely. "Oh, hi," she said. She began quickly reattaching a red leash to the dog's collar.

I couldn't tell if the girl was weirded out by me, my scooter, or both. But I couldn't help myself. I kept talking.

"Your dog," I said, pointing. "Male or female?"

"She's a girl."

"I knew it! This might sound crazy, but she looks *exactly* like my best friend's dog who died. Her name was Lotty."

As soon as I said the word *Lotty*, the Irish setter barked. Seconds later, Winthrop ran over. The two dogs sniffed each other, like dogs do.

Winthrop looked at me with a puzzled expression on his face, as if to say, *Do you see what I see?*

"I mean," I said to the girl, "it's just the weirdest thing. Your dog looks *one hundred percent* like Lotty."

The Irish setter cocked her head and looked at me.

"Lotty?" I said. "Is that you?"

The Irish setter whimpered. Then Winthrop began barking. I took a step closer. "Lotty?"

It was Lotty. Her eyes were the same. Her bark, too. The only difference was this dog seemed a bit more sluggish. Maybe a little depressed.

"I could swear that's my friend's dead dog," I said.

"She's *mine*," the girl said, pulling her dog away with the leash. "And she's one-hundred percent *alive*, thank you very much. We have to go now. Bye."

❧

"Mom, can I borrow your phone?" I asked when I got back to the house.

"No."

"Mom, please. It's important. I have to take some pictures of a dog and send them to Teddy."

"I said no. You and Teddy have had enough fun with cell phones for a while."

Of course, Teddy's mom had told my mom about the DriveMeThere rides. They told each other everything, which was infuriating but not entirely surprising. Teddy and I told each other everything, too.

"Can I at least use your phone to call him?" I asked.

"Use the landline," Mom said. "That's what it's for."

She was still mad about the Mr. Hobart incident. It seemed like Mom was going to be mad at me my whole life.

I left several messages on Teddy's cell phone, hoping he'd call me the minute he got his phone back. Finally, he did, four unbearably long days later.

"Sorry, Ives," he said. "My mom and dad gave me back my phone early, but then I dropped it in the lake. I had to use *rice* to dry it out. It took a couple of days, but now it works like a charm. Isn't that the most bizarre thing? Who would've ever thought to put a phone in a bag of uncooked *rice* when—"

"Teddy, listen," I interrupted. "I don't know how to tell you this, but . . ."

"But what?"

"It's just that I saw, I mean, I *think* I saw, well, I'm ninety-nine percent sure I saw—"

"Spit it out, Ives," Teddy said. "Who'd you see? Melvin Moss?"

"Lotty."

"*What?*"

"I saw Lotty."

"Where? When?"

"In Forest Park. Four days ago. I'm sure it was her."

Teddy didn't believe me at first. *I* didn't believe me at first. But I knew what I saw. Lotty was alive.

"You think Dr. Juniper *cloned* her?" Teddy asked.

"I don't know what to think," I said. "I just know I saw her."

"If you're lying to me, I will never forgive you."

"I might be wrong, but I'm not lying."

"Are you trying to break my heart?"

"Teddy, how can you *ask* me that?"

"My name is Ted."

"Sorry. But seriously, you think I would try to break your heart? I would *never* do that."

Then again, I might be doing that very thing if I was wrong about seeing Lotty. I was either going to be Teddy's best friend or his worst enemy; there was nothing in between. But I had no option. I *had* to tell Teddy I'd seen Lotty in Forest Park. And together, we *had* to find out what Dr. Juniper had done with Teddy's dog.

Just when I'd put the Melvin Moss investigation on hold, here was another mystery nipping at my heels. I felt like the Sherlock Holmes of Magnolia Circle.

What I learned from that:

Being a neighborhood detective was

turning out to be a full-time job.

FIFTEEN

❖

The Bittersweet Vet

When Teddy got back from vacation two days later, we made an appointment to see Dr. Juniper.

"If Dr. Juniper is cloning people's pets without telling them, we have to be careful," said Teddy. "She could be dangerous. Maybe we should wear disguises and think up a fake pet name to use when we call to make the appointment."

I loved Teddy's flair for the dramatic, but the disastrous ladder incident at Mr. Hobart's house burned in my memory. I knew I was still on thin ice with my mom. Teddy had to be careful, too, because of the DriveMeThere rides.

"Let's do this right," I said. "We can use our real names with Dr. Juniper. No sneaking around. No spying. If our parents ask where we're going, we'll just say we're—"

"On a mission!" Teddy said.

"No, that sounds like trouble. We'll say we're doing research about veterinarians. That's true. We'll say we have to interview Dr. Juniper about her clinic."

"Dr. Juniper's *evil* cloning clinic," Teddy added darkly. "Okay, we won't say that part, but I'm thinking it very loudly."

Teddy was jumping to all kinds of conclusions. Meanwhile, I didn't have the heart to tell him I'd been back to Forest Park every day since my initial sighting and I hadn't seen the girl or the Lotty look-alike again. *Was it just my imagination? Was it wishful thinking? Heat stroke?* I would soon find out. We had an appointment with Dr. Juniper for two o'clock the next day.

Teddy and I took the MetroLink train from Skinker Boulevard to Grand Avenue. It wasn't as hard as I thought it'd be with the knee scooter. Teddy was nervous as we rode the elevator up to Dr. Juniper's third-floor office.

"I'm getting a bad feeling about this," he said. "Are you sure you weren't imagining it? Maybe it was a mirage. Maybe you were just *hoping* to see Lotty."

"You have to trust me on this. I know I saw Lotty in the park. I mean, I *think* it was Lotty."

Now I was getting a bad feeling, too.

Dr. Juniper was all crinkly smiles when she greeted us in her office. She was as old as my grammy in Peoria, but not nearly as on the ball. Her white lab coat was covered in pet hair and yellow sticky notes with names and numbers scribbled on them.

"I'm Ted Samuelson," Teddy began. "And this is Ivy Crowden."

"I know who you are," Dr. Juniper said in a friendly voice. She looked at my scooter. "That looks sporty. Have a seat, you two. You're my only appointment this afternoon."

We sat on a clawed-up sofa. There was no receptionist or nurse. Dr. Juniper was a one-woman clinic: veterinarian, nurse, secretary, all rolled into one. You could see how many decades she'd been practicing medicine by the framed pictures of people and pets lining the walls of her waiting room.

Looking at Dr. Juniper surrounded by all the old photos, I was reminded of the word our tour guide had used to describe Scott Joplin's music: *bittersweet*. There was something both happy and melancholy about Dr. Juniper.

She folded her hands on her lap. "I don't see any pets. So what brings you here today?"

I was in no mood to beat around the bush. I told Dr. Juniper I'd seen Lotty in Forest Park.

"I'm positive it was Lotty," I said. "When I called her by name, she responded. She recognized my voice."

I glanced at Teddy sitting next to me. His eyes were already filling with tears. The seriousness of what we were doing was slowly dawning on me. The possible foolishness, too. I was already dreading the train ride back home. Teddy would never forgive me if I was wrong. I would never forgive myself.

"Many Irish setters look alike," Dr. Juniper said cautiously.

"But I *know* it was Lotty," I said, pressing on. "Winthrop recognized her, too. I can't believe all Irish setters *smell* alike."

Dr. Juniper turned and spoke directly to Teddy. "Have you thought about getting a new dog? I know a breeder in Illinois who—"

"I don't *want* a new dog," Teddy said through his tears. "I just want Lotty."

Dr. Juniper bit her lip. Then she tilted back her head and looked at the ceiling. A tear rolled down her cheek.

"It's hard for me, too," she said.

This surprised me. I thought an experienced

veterinarian like Dr. Juniper would be used to the bad parts of her job, like putting down cats and dogs because they had incurable diseases.

Dr. Juniper reached into the pocket of her white lab coat. She pulled out a nylon collar with ID tags.

Teddy's eyes grew wide. "That's Lotty's!"

"Yes, it is," said Dr. Juniper. "Would you like it?"

"Mm-hmm," said Teddy, nodding. He put the collar up to his nose and inhaled deeply. "She's been gone fifty-four days."

Dr. Juniper cleared her throat. It seemed like she was getting ready to make a speech, but then she dropped her gaze to the floor. Her face slid into an upside-down smile.

"I've thought about calling your parents many times," she said, "but I didn't know how to tell them."

"Tell them what?" I said, even though she wasn't talking to me.

Dr. Juniper took a deep breath. "I removed Lotty's collar right before she—"

"I don't want to hear it!" Teddy said, throwing one hand over his eyes. "Please don't say the word *died*."

"Ran away," said Dr. Juniper.

Teddy's hand dropped to his side. "What?"

"Lotty ran away before I could administer the injection."

"Ran away *how*?" I asked. "Where?"

"I have no idea," said Dr. Juniper. "I took off Lotty's collar in the exam room. Then I turned my back for a second to grab the needle, and off she went."

Teddy was on his feet now. "Is there a window? A door? What?"

"The door right there," said Dr. Juniper. She was pointing to the glass office door we'd walked through five minutes earlier. "Lotty jumped from my exam room table and then used her front paws and the weight of her upper body to open the office door. I watched her get on the elevator."

Teddy's face lit up with pride. "Lotty pushed the elevator button?"

"No," said Dr. Juniper. "The elevator door was open. She got on, going down."

"Did you follow her?" I asked.

"Of course I followed her," said Dr. Juniper, defensively. "But it was several minutes before I got down to the lobby. By that time, Lotty was gone. You've seen the lobby of this building. There are six doors. I had no idea which way she went."

Teddy was now pacing around the small

waiting room, gripping Lotty's collar tightly with both hands.

"She had a GPS tracking device on her collar, but she wasn't wearing her collar. Okay, so how else can we find her?"

I turned to Dr. Juniper. "Did you implant a microchip under her fur?"

"Microchip? Is that like a text message? I don't do any of that high-tech stuff."

"Come on, Ives," Teddy said. "We'll find her."

I started to follow Teddy, but Dr. Juniper was holding up her hand like a stop sign.

"Wait," she said. "You're forgetting one thing. Lotty has canine leukemia. It's a terrible disease. I had another dog die from it last week. The family was expecting puppies, and then their beloved dog died without warning. So the chances of Lotty still being alive are not—"

"I *saw* Lotty in the park a week ago," I said. "She looked fine." I reconsidered. "Well, maybe a little older and slower."

"Older and slower," echoed Dr. Juniper, nodding sadly. "It happens to us all."

I didn't know whether to feel sorry for Dr. Juniper or furious with her for being so careless with Lotty. I didn't have time to think about it.

"Let's go, Teddy," I said.

But Teddy was already in the hallway, running toward the elevator. Just like Lotty.

◇◇◇

What I learned from that:

Great minds think alike.

◇◇◇

SIXTEEN

◇◇◇

Group Project

*A*s soon as we got out of Dr. Juniper's office, we started making a plan.

"We have to go to Forest Park and wait for the girl to come back with Lotty," Teddy said. "I'll sleep in the park if I have to. I'll camp out. I don't care if it takes weeks. I don't care if it takes months!"

"May I?" I said, reaching for his cell phone.

I tapped in a search request and read from a website.

"Ninety percent of lost, stray, and unwanted pets in St. Louis end up at one of our four agencies. If your pet is missing, there's a good chance you'll find him or her at one of our shelters. Pets that aren't claimed within thirty days are available for adoption."

I looked up from the phone. Teddy was making a hopeless face and rubbing his eyes.

"No, this is *good*," I said. "Lotty was probably adopted by the girl I saw in the park."

"But how can we find her? And how do we convince the girl to give Lotty back?"

"One thing at a time." I pointed to the phone. "We have to call all four area shelters and describe Lotty. Someone will be able to tell us who adopted her. You take two shelters and I'll take two shelters."

We had to wait until we got back to my house

so I could use the landline. Teddy used his cell phone. We read from the same script.

"Hi, I'm looking for a three-year-old female Irish setter who ran away almost eight weeks ago. She might've ended up at your shelter. If she did, can you please give me the name, address, and phone number of the people who adopted her?"

Five minutes later, all four agencies had told us the same thing: Pet adoptions are private and confidential. No one could confirm or deny if their agency had even sheltered Lotty.

"We're never going to find her," Teddy said.

He was too miserable and stressed to think clearly, but I knew there had to be a way. We'd been in this situation before.

"Melvin," I said.

"What about Melvin?" Teddy asked.

"Who knows more about shelters than Melvin?"

"He knows about homeless shelters for people, not shelters for runaway animals."

"People are animals. Or would you rather I called you a vegetable or a mineral?"

Teddy smiled weakly. He knew I was right.

I called Mrs. Seifert and explained the situation. "My friend Teddy and I are working on a group project and we need Melvin's help. Is there any chance we could see him, just for an hour or two? I promise it has nothing to do with the burglaries or the Trojan sofa. And Mrs. Seifert? A dog's life is at stake."

Mrs. Seifert loved dogs. She had pictures of her golden retriever, Argos, on permanent display all over her classroom. I knew if I wanted

Mrs. Seifert's help, I had to play the dog-in-distress card.

At seven o'clock that night, Mrs. Seifert dropped Melvin off at my house. His hair was still long, but now it was clean and styled. He wore an ironed T-shirt and smelled like Dial soap. Mrs. Seifert didn't mess around.

"I had my second meeting with the police today," Melvin said. "But I'm not allowed to say anything more than that."

That was fine with Teddy and me. We told him we were working on another case. Melvin listened as Teddy recounted our visit to Dr. Juniper's office and our unproductive calls to all four local animal shelters.

"It seems like finding Lotty is harder than finding you," Teddy said. "The worst part is, I don't even know if she's still alive. I wish the universe would give me a sign and let me know she's okay. Just one sign—and I don't want it to be a dead-end sign."

"A sign," Melvin repeated. "We could make signs. You know, with markers and poster board? We could glue on pictures of Lotty and add your phone number for people to call or text if they've seen her."

"That's an excellent idea!" I said. "We'll make the signs and post them all over the park."

Teddy was up and rummaging through the drawers in my living room. "Ives, do you have any markers? Wait, I have some at home. I'll go get them. What about poster board? My sister probably has some we can use."

"I have some poster boards left over from

my Trojan War project." I looked at Melvin. "I mean *our* Trojan War project."

Melvin laughed. "It was your project. I did my own, remember?"

We spent the next hour making more than twenty posters. Teddy's all said the same thing: HAVE YOU SEEN MY DOG? Under the words, he glued a photo of Lotty and wrote his phone number.

I remembered the Latin phrase Dad had taught me: *Primum non nocere.* First, do no harm. On my posters, I wrote: *Primum non nocere.* Pet adoptions are great . . . unless you've adopted a pet who already has a good home. Please do no harm. If you or someone you know has adopted this dog (I glued a picture of Lotty here), contact this number (I wrote Teddy's number here).

Melvin's posters were the simplest. He wrote one word in thick, dark letters across the top of each of his posters: WANTED. Then he added Lotty's photo and Teddy's phone number.

I looked at his clean design and clear message. It was so much better than my show-offy posters with the Latin words.

"That's really good, Melvin," I said. "*Wanted.*"

"*Wanted* sounds like you're looking for a criminal," Teddy said, without looking up from his work.

Melvin was drawing a black border around his poster. "It's the word everyone who runs away wants to hear."

"*Wanted*?" I said.

"You're *wanted*," Melvin explained. "Please come home."

What I learned from that:

*Sometimes all you can do for a
friend who's sad is hope with him
that life gets better.*

SEVENTEEN

◇◇◇

Her Name Is Lotty

The next day, Teddy and I put the posters up all over Forest Park. We duct-taped them to utility poles, park benches, recycling bins, and inside the stalls of public restrooms. I even taped a poster to the front of my knee scooter.

"This will *definitely* get a response," Teddy said. "We just have to wait for the call."

So we waited. No one called or texted the first day.

No one called or texted the second day.

No one called or texted the third day, which was a Friday and the last day of July.

"Tomorrow's Saturday," I told Teddy. "That's the day most people go to the park. Maybe we should go, too. We could ask people if they've seen Lotty."

"Maybe," Teddy said glumly. "Or maybe we should just give up."

He had started to look like a turtle, all hunched over and with a permanent frown on his face.

"You can give up if you want," I said. "*I'm* not giving up."

But on Saturday morning, when I awoke to the sound of heavy rain and thunder, I realized no one would be going to the park that day. And even if they did, our posters would be ruined.

That's when I gave up.

I never should've told Teddy I'd seen Lotty in the park. I didn't mean to, but I had broken his heart a second time. An hour later, I felt sick to my stomach as I pushed my weekend waffle around my syrupy plate.

"That right there is the best waffle I've made all year," Dad said. "And you're not eating it. Would a sliced banana on top help? Whipped cream?"

"I'm not hungry."

Just then the phone rang. It was Teddy.

"I got a text," he said breathlessly. "Can you meet me outside in five minutes? Bring Winthrop—and an umbrella."

I wolfed down my waffle in three bites.

Teddy had memorized the text by the time I got outside. He recited it, under an umbrella, while I read it on his phone.

Saw your poster in the park. My neighbors
adopted an Irish setter. Looks like your dog.
Address is 1801 Costello Ave.

"Costello Avenue is only five minutes away,"
I said. "Come on. We're going!"

Teddy carried my umbrella over his head
while he reread the text message aloud. "Looks
like your dog," he kept saying. "That means
Lotty."

Winthrop barked when he heard Lotty's
name. I just tried to keep up with them on my
knee scooter while trying not to think what
Dr. Ames would say if he saw my cast getting wet
in the rain. I wished I had a cape like Sherlock
Holmes—or even the plastic rain poncho that
was hanging in the coat closet at home.

But there was no turning back now. Our mission was in motion.

The house was a red-brick bungalow with a covered porch. I was hoping Lotty would be outside with the girl I'd seen in the park, but that would've been too easy. We were going to have to knock.

"Please be alive, please be alive, please be alive," Teddy chanted as we walked up the wet porch steps.

I prayed silently. *Please be alive and please be Lotty.* I was glad Winthrop was with us. He would know immediately if the dog in question was his best friend.

Teddy knocked quietly on the door. No one answered.

"Knock harder," I said. "You've got to be louder than the rain."

"I don't want to be rude," he whispered. "Maybe they're not home."

I noticed a black metal doorbell and pushed it. An old-fashioned buzzer sounded, followed by the sound of a dog barking.

"That's her!" Teddy said. "That's Lotty! I'm sure it's her! One hundred percent sure!"

"*Shhhhh*," I said. "Someone's coming."

A girl opened the heavy door. It was the same girl I'd seen in the park. An Irish setter was by her side. We were separated by a screen door so it was hard to see inside, but Winthrop started barking immediately. He was as convinced as Teddy.

"Lotty!" Teddy cried.

I kicked Teddy with my good foot and spoke directly to the girl. "Um, hello. We're sorry to bother you. We wanted to talk about that dog."

"What about my dog?" the girl asked, not opening the screen door.

"Well, the thing is," Teddy began happily, "she's actually *my* dog. Her name is Lotty."

"Her name," said the girl, "is Lucy. And she's my dog. We adopted her from Gateway Shelter. They said someone brought her in off the street. She wasn't wearing a collar."

"That's because our vet took it off," Teddy said. "It's a long story, but basically what happened was—"

"I *wanted* an Irish setter puppy," the girl interrupted. "But they didn't have any at the shelter. All they had was this dog, who isn't very good."

Teddy looked like he'd been punched in the

stomach. "What do you mean Lotty's not very good?"

"Her name is *Lucy*," the girl said. "And she's *not* very good at all. She just lies around all day, like she's a hundred years old."

Lotty was breathing heavily, like she was in pain.

"Lotty?" Teddy said, bending down to look at her through the screen door. "Are you okay?" He stood up again and spoke to the girl at eye level. "Can I pet her?"

The girl heaved a sigh as she pushed open the screen door and pulled Lotty out by the collar onto the porch.

Winthrop's tail wagged frantically at the sight of his old friend. He couldn't resist a curious sniff. But Lotty didn't sniff back. She let out a whine and collapsed in a heap of fur.

The girl sighed again, this time more dramatically. "See what I mean? I had no idea a dog could be this . . . blah."

"Oh, Lotty," said Teddy, falling to his knees and petting her. "Poor Lotty."

Lotty lifted her head to look at Teddy with sad, wet eyes. Then she dropped her chin to the porch floor.

And that's when it happened. Lotty puked.

"She's been doing that all day," the girl grumped. "This is why I wanted a puppy. Puppies pee, but they don't puke. I've never seen a dog as lazy and pukey as Lucy."

"Her name is *Lotty*," Teddy cried. "And she has canine leukemia, okay? So can you cut her a little slack? Just a little slack? Because she probably doesn't have long to live. In fact, she could *die* today, right now, and she probably *will* die if you keep saying *hateful things* in front of her. Yes, she'll probably *die*, just like *you're* going to die someday, and *I'm* going to die someday, and everyone's going to . . ."

I bent down to look at Lotty. Her eyes were rolled back. She was panting heavily. Then she started moaning.

"Teddy," I said, "I don't think Lotty's going to die today. But I think she might be . . . Oh, wow. Yep. She really might be going to . . . Whoa . . . Oh, jeez . . . Yeah, I'd say she's definitely going to—"

"Puppies!" the girl cried. "Lucy's having puppies!"

Teddy was too shocked to correct the girl. He stared at Lotty in slack-jawed awe. Then he handed me his phone.

"Call Dr. Juniper."

What I learned from that:

Some things are impossible

to explain in a phone call.

EIGHTEEN

❖❖❖

Just Like That

*I*t turned out Lotty didn't have canine leukemia after all. What she had was four puppies.

Back in June, Dr. Juniper had mixed up
Lotty's blood work with the other dog whose
family thought she was expecting puppies.
That dog—not Lotty—had tested positive for
canine leukemia. Lotty was in the early days of
pregnancy.

"I think this means it's time for me to retire,"
Dr. Juniper said.

"Please keep your eyes on the road," Teddy said. "We can talk about retirement later."

Dr. Juniper was driving us back to Teddy's house. I was sitting in the front seat with Dr. Juniper. Teddy was in the backseat with Lotty. The new mother was resting in a soft crate with her four squiggly puppies. They were caramel-colored with shiny black noses.

The girl who lived on Costello Avenue—her name was Chloe—was happy to give Lotty back to Teddy, as long as he agreed to give her one of the puppies when they were old enough to be separated from Lotty.

I turned around from the front seat. "Should we see if Melvin wants one of the other puppies?"

"Definitely," said Teddy. "You might have to talk Mrs. Seifert into it. Tell her if there were a Cute Puppy Olympics—and why isn't there one, by the way?—these four puppies would *all* win gold medals."

I laughed. I knew Melvin would love a puppy, and it wouldn't be hard to convince Mrs. Seifert, given her love of dogs.

Dr. Juniper parked in front of Teddy's apartment building. "I'll help you get the dogs inside. I owe your family an explanation."

"Come on up," Teddy said. "We're on the fourth floor. Are you coming, too, Ives?"

"No," I said. "I'm not up for all those stairs. Plus, I need to dry out my cast with a hair dryer."

Both things were true, but I also couldn't wait to get home and tell my parents the good news.

"Teddy got Lotty back?" Dad asked, an hour later when he came home from work. "Just like that?"

"Not just like that," Mom said. "Just like *that*." She was pointing at me. "Ivy tracked down Lotty like an old-fashioned detective."

"It was a group project," I said. "Melvin Moss had the idea to make posters."

Mom turned to Dad. "Diane Samuelson called and told me the whole story. It might've been a group effort, but Ivy was the mastermind."

Mastermind. It was the word Teddy and I had used to describe Mr. Hobart. It reminded me of the apology letter I'd written, and my promise to be a better neighbor.

I told Mom and Dad about Lotty's four puppies.

"Dr. Juniper said they need to stay with Lotty

for eight weeks. Then they can go to their new homes. Chloe is getting one. Melvin's getting one. Teddy's family is keeping one."

"That leaves one puppy," Dad said with a sly smile.

Mom lifted an eyebrow. "Puppies are a whole *lot* of work."

"They're a whole lot of cuteness, too," I said.

"I don't think you remember when Winthrop was a puppy," Mom said. "We had to teach him everything."

"I know," I said. "But it was worth it. Can you imagine our family without Winthrop?"

Hearing his name, Winthrop woke up and sauntered over to where I was sitting. He flopped down in front of me, resting his head on my foot.

"I vote in favor of a puppy," Dad said.

Mom's skeptical face shifted into a reluctant smile. "I guess I vote for a puppy, too."

I took a breath. I had to say it fast before I changed my mind.

"I was thinking maybe we could give the puppy to Mr. Hobart. I could walk the puppy before and after school, when I walk Winthrop. Don't you think a puppy would be good for Mr. Hobart?"

Mom put her index finger to her lips. "I think," she said in a quivery voice, "a puppy would be wonderful for Mr. Hobart, if you're willing to help him take care of it."

"I am," I said. "I'll do everything—feeding, walking, brushing."

"Well, one thing is clear," Dad said. "We need to find a new vet. We're not going back to Dr. Juniper, that's for sure."

"Tomorrow," Mom said. "We'll look for a new vet tomorrow. Right now I want to bask in the pride I feel for our girl."

⬦⬦⬦

What I learned from that:

I wish I could bottle what it feels like to make my parents proud. I'd take a sip of it every day.

⬦⬦⬦

NINETEEN

◇◇◇

Boy Wins Lottery—
Twice

A reporter for the *St. Louis Post-Dispatch* found out what happened and called Teddy's family to set up an interview. The article, which included a photo of Teddy with Lotty and the puppies, ran ten days later on the front page of the newspaper. The headline used Lotty's full name.

BOY CLAIMS HE WON LOTTERY TWICE

(VET SAYS LOTTERY WON BOY)

In the article, Dr. Juniper told the whole story about the mix-up with the lab work and how Lotty had escaped from her office. She also announced her retirement.

Teddy ran over to my house with the paper. "Did you see the story in the newspaper?"

"Yeah," I said. "It's a great picture of you!"

"Not that story. This story."

He opened the newspaper and showed me an article at the top of page five.

St. Louis Post-Dispatch · Tuesday, August 11

CRIME WAVE OVER, SAYS POLICE CHIEF

ST. LOUIS—St. Louis Police Chief Sam MacPherson says residents can take comfort that a recent crime wave has been solved.

Two men, Jason Pipley and Josiah Callin, were arrested and charged yesterday on two counts of burglary. The first incident took place in June on Magnolia Circle when the men allegedly posed as sofa deliverymen. The second burglary on Washington Avenue occurred less than a week later when the same men allegedly repeated the crime. In both cases, authorities say a ten-year-old runaway boy hidden in a sofa crawled out from a secret compartment and stole money and jewelry from the apartments.

"We're not revealing the name of the boy, for his protection," said Police Chief MacPherson. "But we couldn't have solved these crimes without him. He came forward voluntarily and explained his role in the burglaries. He said Pipley and Callin approached him at a downtown homeless shelter and said they'd turn him over to authorities if he didn't act as an accomplice."

MacPherson said the runaway boy will face no legal consequences for his participation in the crimes. "We're trying to find a long-term foster home for the boy. The situation he's in now is temporary."

According to MacPherson, St. Louis residents should always be on alert for anything that seems unusual in their neighborhood.

"The tried-and-true advice holds," said MacPherson. "If you see something, say something. You could be saving a neighbor's favorite pearl necklace or a runaway child's life."

"We should frame this for Melvin," I said.

"That's a great idea," said Teddy. He was looking at the newspaper and frowning. "I just wish it had a picture of Melvin."

"They *can't* show his picture. Those two thugs have friends who would hurt Melvin for talking to the police."

"Oh, that's right," Teddy said. He folded the

newspaper carefully. "So, Ives, I have some great news."

"Tell me."

"Well," he began, "you know how the article says Melvin's living situation is temporary? That's because Mrs. Seifert and her husband can't keep Melvin past October."

"Why not?"

"They're not certified to be foster parents. But guess who might be in a few weeks."

"Who?"

"My parents," said Teddy. "Daphne's leaving for college in a week, so Melvin can have her room. We'll be his foster family until his mom gets out of rehab."

"*What*? Seriously?"

"Yeah," said Teddy. "My parents have to fill out a bunch of paperwork. Then someone has to come inspect our apartment. But the social worker said it's ninety-nine percent a sure thing."

"Wow. That's fantastic."

Somehow it didn't feel fantastic to me. Melvin Moss had always been in my homeroom. He was my friend before he was Teddy's friend. We were Trojan War project partners—for one day, anyway. If Melvin Moss was going to live in anyone's house, he should live in my house.

After a few hours, the jealous feeling passed. Of course Melvin should live with Teddy's family. It made sense.

But Melvin didn't end up needing Daphne's room. We found out a few days later that Melvin's mom was scheduled to be released in October from the drug rehab clinic.

Melvin was going home—with a puppy.

What I learned from that:

Corny as it sounds, there's

no place like home.

TWENTY

◇◇◇

I Love Stairs

When the piano arrived on Friday morning, Dad was practically jumping out of his skin with excitement.

"After I learn how to play," he said, "I'm going to learn how to compose music. I want to write some modern ragtime tunes. Hey, maybe I'll compose the 'Magnolia Circle Rag.'"

"In the meantime," Mom said, "are you free to join Ivy and me? We have an appointment with Dr. Ames."

"Sure," said Dad.

So we went as a family—Mom, Dad, and me. A technician removed my cast so I could have another round of X-rays. Then we waited in an examining room.

"Good, good, good," Dr. Ames said as he strode into the room. "I see you've brought the whole family to your graduation."

"Graduation?" I said.

"That's what I call it," Dr. Ames replied. "You've put in the hard work of recovery. I know it hasn't been easy, but I hope you found a way to make the most of your time."

"Did she ever!" Dad said. He spent the next five minutes bragging to Dr. Ames about how I'd "rescued" Melvin Moss and tracked down Lotty "like an old-fashioned detective." (I had finally come clean and told my parents all the details about both cases, once the investigations had been successfully completed.)

Mom interrupted Dad to ask Dr. Ames about my leg. "So she doesn't need to keep using the knee scooter?"

"No," said Dr. Ames. "Our work here is done. Ivy can resume all normal activities."

"*Really*?" I said.

"Really," he said.

"Is there anything she can't do?" Mom asked. "Anything she should avoid?"

"Just be sensible," said Dr. Ames. He turned to me and smiled. "And be careful of stairs, Ivy. I know how you hate them."

"Oh, I don't hate stairs anymore."

"You don't?" asked Dr. Ames.

"No way. If it weren't for stairs, I wouldn't have broken my leg. And if I hadn't broken my leg, I wouldn't have been stuck in a cast all summer. And if I hadn't been stuck in a cast all summer, I wouldn't have been looking out the window and seen Melvin Moss getting in a white van. And . . . well, it's a long story, but I think stairs are the perfect symbol for life."

"Why is that?" said Dr. Ames, grinning.

"Because they represent the ups and downs of life. So, no, I don't hate stairs. I *love* stairs. I love them so much, I'm going to marry stairs."

On the drive home, I told Mom and Dad I had been acting silly with Dr. Ames instead of showing what I was really feeling.

"What are you really feeling?" Mom asked.

"Happy."

"We're happy you're happy," Dad said. "It wasn't such a terrible summer, was it?"

"Not at all."

What I didn't say, because it would've sounded too cheesy, was that it was the best summer of my life. Dr. Ames was right. I thought having a broken leg would mean my world was going to get smaller, but it didn't. Even with a broken leg, life could still be big and fun and wonderful, as long as you had a best friend and a best dog.

And look at me! I had Teddy and Winthrop and Lotty and Melvin Moss and Mrs. Seifert. I even had Mr. Hobart, who decided to name his puppy Maggie, short for Magnolia Circle.

My summer had been just like my street. At first it seemed like a dead end, but there had been room to turn around. Maybe that's why Magnolia Circle never did get a dead-end sign.

There was always plenty of room on our street to turn around.

The next day, homeroom assignments arrived in the mail. Teddy and I sat on the front steps of my house and opened the envelopes slowly.

"Who'd you get?" Teddy asked ominously.

"Ms. Queset," I said. "You?"

"Ms. Queset!" Teddy yelled.

By some miracle, we were in the same homeroom. It was the first time since first grade. Better still, we were in Ms. Queset's room.

Ms. Blanche Queset was a legend at our school. Everybody wanted to be in her class because she let fifth graders choose their own community service projects and work independently or in groups.

"I wonder who Melvin got," Teddy said. "I'm going to call him."

Melvin was also in Ms. Queset's homeroom. It was definitely a miracle—or more likely, an act of divine intervention by Mrs. Seifert.

Later that day, Teddy and I met Melvin in Forest Park. He didn't know anything about Ms. Queset, so we told him how lucky we all were to have her for fifth grade.

"Hey, Melvin," I said, "what would you think about working together on our community service project? You, me, and Teddy?"

"That'd be cool," he said.

"We could design a new roller coaster for Six Flags," I said. "Or invent a new flavor of frozen custard. Or you could teach us how to build furniture with secret compartments."

"We could find a cure for canine leukemia,"

Teddy said. "And start the Cute Puppy Olympics!"

"We could solve crimes in St. Louis," Melvin said.

"Why not all over the country?" I asked.

"The world!" Melvin said, laughing.

"Are you up for that, Ted?" I asked.

Finally, I remembered to call him Ted instead of Teddy.

Melvin looked at Teddy with a puzzled expression. "So are you going by 'Ted' now?"

"Nah," Teddy said with a wave of his hand. "Maybe in middle school, but not fifth grade. Can't we still be kids for a while?"

"Yes!" Melvin and I cried at the same second.

Of course, I wanted to grow up. I *yearned* to be old enough so I could get my own phone and credit card and DriveMeThere account.

But I also wished I could slow down time so summer could go on and on. I didn't want it to end. Not summer. Not calling Teddy "Teddy." Not this perfect day. Not being a kid. Not this *journey*, as Dr. Ames would call it, or the weirdly fun habit of writing down things I learned along the way.

My eyes filled with bittersweet tears as I understood, in a new way, what Scott Joplin meant in the instructions he wrote for his piano compositions. I ran and laughed and yelled at the top of my lungs on that late summer day: "*Do not play this piece fast!*"

What I learned from that:

If you have more than one friend

and one dog in your life, you've won

the lottery. If you don't have at least

one friend or one dog, turn it around.

Turn it around.

ACKNOWLEDGMENTS

When I was about Ivy's age, I spent a summer vacation with my arm in a cast. I remember the painful fall from the jungle gym that caused the break, the maddening itch of the plaster cast against my skin, and the party I had the day the cast was finally removed. But the nuts and bolts of how my bones healed under the cast? I didn't remember or understand any of that until I sat down to write this book. That's when I got to ask all of my (and Ivy's) questions to two medical experts: Dr. Paul M. Olive, an ortho-pedic surgeon in Springfield, Missouri, and Erik

Heinzen, a general surgery physician assistant in Denver, Colorado. Both were unfailingly generous with their time and knowledge. All of the medical wisdom in this novel comes from them. Any fractured facts are mine.

Thanks, too, to my beloved editor, Liz Szabla, who planted the seed for this book one evening when we were discussing Alfred Hitchcock's movie *Rear Window*. We wondered if it might be possible to create a similar mystery starring a ten-year-old girl whose secret strength lies in her kindness, curiosity, and love of animals.

My secret strength is my circle of friends who make my life better every day. I'm looking at you, Joyce McMurtrey, Sherry Huffman, and Jeannette Olsen. Other friends will find their names embedded in the narrative. Yes, that's you, Taylor (and Karma) Mathews, Daryl

Steen, Uma Hiremath, "Doctor" Bill Ames, and Mrs. (Lex Anne) Seifert.

Writing a work of fiction always feels to me like climbing a mountain alone in the dark without a map or a flashlight. In real life, I'm lucky to have someone who helps me navigate the ups and downs of this world. I really *do* love stairs and mountains and you, Roger Kaza.

−Kate